A FAE'S WISHMAS

KIRA NYTE

AUTHOR NOTE

Dear Reader,

Cat's Paw Cove is a magical town dreamed up by Wynter Daniels and Catherine Kean, a charming seaside paradise where cats are king, and anything is possible. We are so excited to bring you not only our own stories, but also contributions from an incredibly talented group of Guest Authors. With paranormal and mystery romance, time travel, and more, there's something for everyone. We hope you'll enjoy reading the series as much as we enjoy writing it. For more information about the Cat's Paw Cove series, please visit http://CatsPawCoveRomance.com.

Happy reading!

Wynter Daniels & Catherine Kean

A FAE'S WISHMAS

Woodland fae Niera travels the world finding the Fated matches of humans and paranormal creatures alike. The Mystical Matchmaker has brought ninety-nine couples together, but her own happiness remains elusive. A friend's call for help brings her to Cat's Paw Cove just in time to learn she must make a one-hundredth match or spend the rest of her days alone.

The unsuspecting humans in the magical enclave have no idea that easygoing surfing instructor Alistair has been trapped on land by a curse. Worse, the town's mysterious Sherwood cats seem to have conspired for decades to thwart his battle to return to the sea every full moon.

Niera's business is love, but she hardens her heart when she meets the gorgeous man with indigo eyes and too many secrets. Confident Alistair feels as clumsy as a youth whenever the beautiful, compassionate fae looks his way.

Neither have room in their lives for romance—until a meddling little calico sticks her paw in to do some match-making of her own.

CHAPTER ONE

If anyone told her she'd find herself in some flat little seaside town far from the comfort of forests and mountains, she'd have laughed until fruits fell from the trees and the birds warbled, begging her to stop.

Alas, she found herself resisting the idea of continuing down a street seemingly littered not only with humans and magical creatures poorly disguised by glamour, but with *cats*.

Niera Blair shifted the linen bag to her right shoulder, clutching the straps with both hands. The briny scent of seawater assaulted her nostrils while the salt coming off the choppy waters coated her skin in a sticky residue. It took the might of a thousand dryads to keep from twisting her face in horror. Somehow she managed, pushing aside her utter dismay with vivid memories of the pristine forests she'd hiked, the cozy caves she'd set up living quarters in when the weather turned treacherous, the critters, the birds, the wild fruits and the smell of clean earth. Forests held an untamed essence, a vivacious energy that sang to her soul and fed her body with life.

Here, not so much. The heavy air siphoned strength from

her muscles and sapped that life from her spirit, like salt on a mushroom cap.

Darn sea fae.

"Annise, all because I adore you as a friend," she groaned as a gust of wind knocked into her side, casting her hair across her face and causing her to stumble a few steps.

Strong hands caught her arms, steadying her on her feet as she raked the unruly locks away from her eyes. Her skin tingled, a strange and alien sensation, starting where those hands made contact on her bare skin and slowly spreading over her flesh.

She recoiled from the warm touch, unnerved. *What in the sweet gods' names...*

"Careful there."

Tucking rebel strands of hair behind her ears as the wind calmed, she lifted her gaze to the face of the utterly handsome man whose deep indigo eyes watched her with a mixture of wonder and curiosity. Ash-blond hair brushed over his forehead in the waning breeze, making him appear boyish in torn-at-the-knees blue jeans and a white V-neck sweater. Two men around his age approached his back, laughing, arms slung around each other.

One guy clapped a hand on his shoulder, giving Niera a shameless once-over before tugging her savior away.

"C'mon, bud. We're gonna be late." The newcomer mimed a tip of an invisible hat and mocking bow. "G'day, m'lady."

Niera blinked as the three men hustled away. Her arms still tingled and her blood felt like someone had infused it with Pop Rocks, those annoying little sizzling candies she'd been tricked into trying by a nymph during her last matchmaking adventure.

The man tossed a lingering glance over his shoulder, his

mouth curling in a close-lipped smile, eyes twinkling in the glaring sunlight. His steps resisted the pull of his friend's hand, but he continued on, finally turning from her and settling into an easy stride to an unknown destination.

Niera rubbed her arms where his hands had touched her, trying in vain to disperse the heat that suffused her skin.

Tugging her cell phone from her cross-over bag—she had a tenuous relationship with modern technology, since she didn't care for it and it didn't seem to like her in return— Niera pulled up Annise's number.

With her arrival in Cat's Paw Cove, her mood turned dour and her energy ebbed. Something about the small town sucked the life from her faster than she could refill her reserves, something uncanny. She didn't care for seaside towns at the best of times, since the magic of sea fae tended to dominate the energy, but something malicious was at work. Something that needled who she was, *what* she was, and wanted her gone.

Happy to oblige, trust me. As soon as I finish what I came here for.

Her friend answered on the third ring with a cheery, "Tell me you've arrived!"

"Oh, I'm here, all right. But here doesn't seem to like me much," Niera said, gauging her surroundings. The Uber driver had dumped her off at the corner of Tabby Road *—Given the population of felines, it makes sense, I suppose—* and left without so much as a goodbye.

Oh, to return to the woodland life.

"Poppycock, silly. You'll fit right in, just wait and see."

Niera scoffed. She'd wait, but so far, she wasn't seeing much promise. "Sure. Okay, so I'm at Tabby Road and"—she looked around for a landmark—"Sherwood? There's a hotel behind—oh, I guess that's where I'm supposed to stay."

"Ah, yes! The Catnip Hotel. Never mind that. I'll come fetch you and you'll stay with me. It'll be much nicer, and we can get our quality time in before you vanish, gypsy style."

Niera sighed to herself. The hotel wasn't in shambles, which was a step up from her last overnight accommodations. She didn't care for the nearness to the ocean, nor the uneasy air that tangled her spirit into a knot. She'd booked a single night at the hotel, intent on testing the proverbial waters. The woman responsible for reservations assured her there were plenty of vacancies during her expected stay.

That never boded well.

With a resigned shrug, she twisted around, noting the town hall nearby, flanked by the fire station and police station. "Okay, sure. That might be better."

"Yas!" Her friend's high-pitched squeal of pleasure made Niera cringe. Gods, she really needed some nature time if she hoped to keep her temper under control. "Great! Follow Sherwood down to Whiskers, make a right, and you'll come to Calico Court. I'll meet you at the Cove Cat Café in ten." Another squeal made Niera pull the phone from her ear. "Oh, I'm so happy!"

"Ah, yes. So am I. Definitely happy to see you."

She ended the call and tucked her phone into her bag. Her shoulders slumped and she gripped the straps. Of their own accord, her eyes turned down Sherwood Boulevard, in the direction of the ash-haired man and his two friends. Foolish to think he'd be waiting for her somewhere up the road. Foolish to believe the gods would ever grant her a man of her own.

No.

They'd gifted her with a knack for finding everyone else a perfect match. A perfect mate. Her talents were whispered far and wide. She answered calls and inquiries through emails, traveling here and there to try and find some lonely creature their one true love.

It wasn't easy at times. Heck, it wasn't easy *most* of the time. But the moment two people came together and that spark flared?

It made all her efforts worth the struggle.

Those of inhuman origins called her the Mystical Matchmaker, while those without magical abilities considered her a miracle worker.

All in all, she had the gift to make everyone around her happy—and lacked all the power in the world to experience that happiness herself.

Here she stood, at the corner of Tabby and Sherwood, the sea at her back assaulting her senses, answering the call of her friend.

For Annise, she'd swim across that wretched sea, face down the sea fae and their belligerence, all for the sake of making her friend happy.

She'd do her part, do what she did best. Hopefully make her one-hundredth match and avoid catastrophe.

Somewhere in Cat's Paw Cove resided a male placed on this Earth for her friend alone. Annise swore she'd found him, a man she started dating only a couple of weeks ago, but who was, without a doubt, her mate.

Niera just had to confirm the match before the prophetic dream from last night came to fruition.

Before the first snowflake fell from the sky.

Before all hope of future happiness for her was lost, and her gift became a curse.

ALISTAIR CUMMINGS GLANCED OVER HIS SHOULDER FOR THE umpteenth time, pining after the strange woman with the mahogany hair and shocking honey eyes. He had no explanation for why he felt so drawn to the stranger except for her attractive petite frame and almost pixie-like features, and something in the energy that poured off her skin.

He'd crossed a few pixies in his time at Cat's Paw Cove. His friend was dating one, or so Alistair believed. She definitely had something faery-ish about her.

"Hey, bud, where you at?"

Brayden Conner knocked him in the shoulder, jolting his thoughts from the woman. The sweet briny air called to him like the sun on his skin, cocooning him in its embrace. He lived for the water, the ocean, the waves. Lived for the feel of salt on his skin and the rightness of the blue abyss. He passed most of his days paddling on a surfboard or diving around the reefs, waiting for the day he could return to his home.

"Right here with you," Alistair said, flashing his friend an unwavering smile. "Think we'll have full classes today with the dip in the temperature?"

Brayden shrugged one of his thick shoulders and smirked. "Dude, we'll make good use of the time on the water. Always do." His dark brows shot up beneath his dark spill of shaggy bangs, flattened by the baseball cap he wore like a teen. "Why?" He wagged those brows. "Chick got your tongue?"

Alistair laughed. "Yeah, like that'll happen. I broke my own record with the last gal, making it four months before she took off. Women in the age bracket I'm looking for don't care for beach bums."

"Maybe you need to divulge your reasons for being beach bum material." Brayden twirled a hand in the air, cutting him off before he could mutter a word of comment or protest. "Then again, they wouldn't understand."

And therein lay the problem he faced with every relationship, or attempted relationship.

Women wanted men with secure jobs. Financially-fit futures.

All he could offer was the promise of happiness, protection, and a life by the ocean, and it would only be a temporary life, at that.

He never divulged his history to anyone, including his friends. He kept his funds—what wasn't tucked away in the reefs—safely hidden at the local bank. His friends speculated where his money came from, casually teasing him about a trust fund or an impressive lottery win. They had no idea what he concealed from them.

"Know her?" Brayden asked, shooting a look over his own shoulder. "Haven't seen her in these parts."

"Between tourists and newcomers, I don't keep up. But no." He'd never forget a woman like her. "Never seen her before."

"Hmm. Wonder if she's hanging around for a bit. Maybe we can track her down after the minnows class."

What he'd give to track his way back to her now. His fingers stung, and not unpleasantly. Actually, they prickled and tingled in a way that urged him to backtrack, find the woman, and connect with her skin again—a touch, a simple caress, something that might quench the burn beneath his skin. No degree of tension he applied in an attempt to rub away the sensation seemed to work.

It flared to life when he stopped her stumble in the wind.

She'd have knocked right into him had he not caught her, and in that brief and unexpected encounter, he wanted to pull her close.

So strange, all things considered.

Shaking his head, hoping the brewing fantasies in his

head would subside—he may be a thing of lore, but he sure wasn't a believer in Fate and all that mumbo jumbo—he rolled out his shoulders and put a little spunk in his step.

The ocean released another brutal gust, one that swept his hair back from his face, made his eyes squint, and a smile peel across his mouth. Brine, that sea-sweet flavor, spread over his tongue and settled in his lungs, a familiar infusion he lusted for every morning when he woke.

He had two more nights until the peak of the full moon. Two more nights to endure before he could set himself free in the dark ebb and flow of the midnight tide.

But in Cat's Paw Cove, two nights could equal two decades, if he crossed the wrong person or stumbled across a "misplaced" portal.

Every month, that seemed to be what happened, and it always occurred at the mischievous paws of the Sherwood cats.

CHAPTER TWO

"*Y*ou *what*?!"

Niera gawked at Annise from across the small café table. She didn't give a rabbit's tail fluff about the coffee that had dribbled down her chin and splattered on the tabletop and floor, but apparently one of the calico cats had no problem stretching its lean body to lap at the droplets. Annise laughed, but her face turned beet red, highlighting the spattering of freckles over the bridge of her otherwise pale nose. Bright red hair fell over her cheeks when she looked down at her tangled fingers.

"Annise, I didn't come here to make matches for the masses. I came here to help *you*."

Her voice, low and hissy, wrung a sigh from her friend. She'd met Annise a few years back on a ranch while she was matching a down-on-his-luck bull rider and a lonely elementary school teacher who'd given up any hope of finding love. Annise had been a ranch hand with a suspicious ability to make the farm animals do her bidding.

Niera noticed immediately the pixie's magic, and vice

versa. Since then, they'd built a friendship over impromptu trips, magical festivities, and mischief.

This was so *not* Niera's kind of mischief. It was one-sided, and not favoring her side at all!

"You know the ocean steals my energy. I can't stay here long without consequences."

"You won't have to stay long, I promise! Listen, this is a magical time of year. Cat's Paw Cove is brimming with holiday cheer."

She hadn't noticed the snowflake banners and strings of unlit lights wrapped around every streetlight pole, tree trunk, and vertical surface she'd passed. Nor had she gaped at both colorful and rustic style garlands draped around storefronts, dripping with holiday décor that sparkled in the sunlight.

Nope. Not at all.

"Christmas in this town is special. Just imagine all the happiness you can bring the residents by helping them find their perfect matches." Annise splayed her hands to emphasize *perfect matches* and smiled, but concern washed any hope of that smile reaching her eyes. "And I only told a few people."

"No." Niera finally opted for the paper napkin, startling the cat lapping at the drops of coffee, and wiped her chin. "I offered *you* my help. You said there's someone here that caught your fancy, and I came to see if he compliments you. I'm not spending more time in this seaside town than I have to. I'm not Cupid."

"I know. I've met Cupid. Or someone very close to a cupid." Annise shook her vibrant head and snickered. "You're definitely not her. And your abilities are different."

"I match those the Fates have decided to weave together. I can't just"—Niera made a sharp pull and push motion with her fists—"put people together."

With an exasperated sigh, she dropped her hands on the table, causing the coffee mugs to clatter against the surface. Her gaze lowered to the cat that sat on its haunches and stared up at her with green eyes. Its tail swooshed back and forth over the floor. Unusual markings that resembled a mask surrounded its gleaming eyes.

"And the thing with the cats in this town is weird. They're everywhere. I prefer rabbits and fawns."

"Niera, they're not all normal cats."

"We're both stubborn creatures."

Annise dropped back against her chair and snorted. "That I won't argue, but the cats here are different. You'll see." She jutted her chin at the calico. "Seems you've got your first furry friend there."

Niera raised a brow at the cat, which earned her a rumbling purr, followed by what she could only describe as a feline smile. A white-toed paw stretched up to her thigh, tapped tentatively against her jean-clad leg, then came to rest there.

"You can stop playing marionette with the kitty, Annise. It's not smoothing things over, I promise you." She started to take the cat's paw and remove it from her leg when its sandpaper-like tongue brushed her arm. Gods, she could have sworn the animal smiled. And those eyes held far too much understanding to be a simple cat. "Seriously."

"I'm not doing anything. Couldn't even if I wanted to. I told you, these cats aren't normal cats." She flicked a finger toward the animal. "However, I can tell you she's rather fond of you."

"Annise is right, you know."

Niera's head snapped up to see a pretty woman approaching their table, blond hair tied up in a ponytail. She wore a bright smile as she leaned down and scooped the cat into her arms, earning a soft meow and a pleased purr. The cat's eyes settled at half-mast as her ears were scratched.

"I'm Jordan. I help Luna out at the café, placing the kitties with families. And this one here"—she nuzzled the cat's nose with her own—"escaped the kitty room."

"Nice to meet you," Niera said, shedding her frustration over Annise's decision to promote her matchmaking gift without her approval.

"This one here is Holly and she loves the outdoors. She never strays far, is loyal and very well-behaved."

Jordan nuzzled Holly's furry tri-colored head, winning twitching whiskers and another feline grin. Niera's brows pinched as she considered the expression. She'd witnessed plenty of forest animals express happiness through grins, but this cat seemed to understand exactly what they were discussing and *reacted* appropriately.

Jordan lifted her head from Holly's and shared that beaming smile again. "Annise told me you enjoy nature. Holly here would be a wonderful companion for you."

Niera opened her mouth to politely refuse, but Annise shot up in her chair and nodded.

"Niera needs a companion."

"Um, Annise, I live a nomadic lifestyle. Surely a cat would want a place to settle down and call her own." Oh, mental slap. Why on Earth was she talking about a cat as she would a potential match? "Besides, I spend much of my time hiking and camping and, you know"—Niera glowered at her friend, silently reminding her she preferred forests over houses—"being away from home."

"Well," Jordan began, placing Holly back on the floor. The cat stretched her back, tail flicking languidly in the air, and settled at Niera's feet. Jordan lifted her brows. "Let me know if you change your mind. She appears pretty set on staying with you."

The woman hustled away, scooping up another cat from the sofa as she headed to room off the main area of the shop. A dozen or more cats, seen through a large window, were draped, sprawled, or stretched out over all surfaces within this cat room.

Annise leaned over the table in a conspiratorial manner, excitement glowing in her eyes. "Jordan's a cat whisperer. She can talk to cats and they talk to her."

"Like you."

"No. I can't actually *speak* with animals. It's more of an understanding of their emotions and a connection with them."

Niera nodded, fighting the pull to look down at Holly. Part of her spirit wanted to ignore the softening she felt toward the creature while her logical inner voice reminded her she was in no way, shape, or form equipped to take in a domesticated animal. It wasn't that she disliked cats or dogs, but they needed stability. Shelter, food, water, vet care. Niera believed animals belonged in the wild, free to live as they chose, but understood many domesticated breeds would never survive.

How would Niera handle being tied to one place, her freedoms leeched?

I'd shrivel up and disappear.

Not literally, but she'd become nothing more than a shell of a fae.

Returning to her coffee, she sipped the lukewarm drink. "Tell me about this guy you want me to investigate for you."

Annise's entire demeanor shifted to what Niera could only describe as star-struck.

"Oh, Niera, wait until you meet him. He's handsome and kind and has a sense of humor that'll make your sides stitch from laughing so hard. He's so carefree and easygoing. Loves the ocean, but also maintains a garden at his house. He's so perfect that I can't possibly imagine him *not* being my match." Annise's eyes rolled to the ceiling as she sighed dreamily. "He's got this dimple on the right side of his mouth that is utterly fascinating when he smiles."

"When do you want me to meet him?"

The sooner, the better.

There was only so much sea she could handle, as evidenced by her increasingly gloomy mood. The poor temper was completely at odds with her usual kind, gentle, and loving self.

"He's teaching a class right now, but is usually done by two. I can settle you in at my place in the meantime."

Settling in wouldn't take long. She always packed light, not that her wardrobe extended beyond a couple pairs of jeans, T-shirts, sweatshirts, and sneakers. She replaced her few simple possessions as needed.

"We're planning on meeting up before the Christmas Parade and grabbing some pizza slices from Pie in the Sky. It'll be a real casual way for you to meet him for the first time."

"Sounds like a plan," Niera said, finishing her coffee in one large gulp.

A worried crease furrowed Annise's brow and her smile dimmed. "I know how much you hate the ocean. You told me that your fae blood repels it, for either magical reasons or personal. We can stop at Eye of Newt next door. It's a really neat metaphysical shop. There might be something to help you counter the effects." Her friend reached across the table and grabbed her hands. "Having you agree to come here means the world to me. I can't tell you how much I appreciate it, how much our friendship means. You always strive to make everyone around you happy. I'm not blind to the fact that it takes a toll on you. You know, maybe this Christmas you should put others aside and consider your own happiness."

Niera turned her hands over in Annise's grip and squeezed her friend's fingers. Annise's heartfelt words filled her with adoration, a reminder of why she would do anything for the pixie.

"I've never been good at finding someone to compliment me. My gift extends to others. I can't use it on myself. Seeing happiness form between two people fills me with my own sense of completion."

And disappointment, but she'd never admit that to anyone. Giving so much of herself to others depleted her until she replenished her magic and energy with a respite in the forest. It was one of the main reasons it had taken her almost thirty years to the day to complete the Fates' honored— though she didn't consider it honored when failure to complete one-hundred matches by the last day of the twenty-ninth year would leave her cursed to loneliness for eternity —assignment.

Annise patted the backs of her hands and drew away, a touch of deviousness crossing her pretty face. "Well, maybe this is your year. Your season. Your Christmas for a wish to come true."

Niera dredged up a smile and a lighthearted laugh. "You know as well as I do that's not how things work with me. I can wish for love all I want, but that love manifests itself between two other people, never me and a possible match."

Holly tapped Niera's ankle with her paw, the touch gentle, almost soothing. Reluctantly, she looked down at the pretty cat, currently on her back, belly exposed, hind legs stretched out like she owned the floor. Those green eyes peered up at her with more understanding than she'd ever expect to see in a domesticated animal. A twinkle, like she knew exactly what bothered Niera, and held the secret to solving her dilemma.

"Whatever. I propose a challenge to you. But first"— Annise pushed her empty coffee mug away and stood up —"let's get you something to ward off the effects of the ocean and get a glimpse of your future."

NIERA LIFTED HER BROWS AT THE CALICO CAT SAUNTERING along at her heel. Whether the cat was a wanderer and the café didn't mind her coming and going as she pleased was a mystery. However, Holly's determination to keep close to Niera both warmed an empty space in her chest and seemed to keep the effects of the ocean at bay.

A little.

Strange.

The doorbell jingled overhead as Annise pulled open the glass door to Eye of Newt. Niera half expected to walk into a witch's den. Her fae blood immediately latched onto the magic that sifted through the air. Serene energy surrounded her, the essences changing like gentle, unseen waves. It called to the magic infusing her spirit, emboldening her with the confidence she'd lost when her driver left her on the side of the road to be pummeled by briny ocean air.

Annise locked her fingers around Niera's wrist and dragged her toward the back of the store, waving to a handsome man straightening some bottles of essential oils on a shelf by the register.

"Hi, Eli. Is Emma here?"

The man nodded and motioned to a thick beaded curtain

that hid everything beyond it from view. "She's not with a client, so go ahead back."

Niera leaned close to her friend and whispered, "What are we doing?"

"*We* are going to say hi to Emma. *You* are going to get a glimpse into your future."

"My what? Wait, what—"

The beads parted with a clack and whoosh, a sound that reminded Niera of rain dripping through tree branches. An older woman popped her head out. Behind her, Niera could see an eccentric room cast in dim illumination and the flickers of candlelight. Wild, wide black eyes darted between her and Annise until they narrowed on Niera. She huffed a breath, a black curl fluttering from her tanned cheek.

"You. Oh, yes, you." She snickered, straightened her shoulders, and waved Niera into the room. When Annise urged her forward and started to follow, the woman tsked. "No, child. Just the woodland fae." Her dark gaze dropped to Holly. "And the kitty."

Niera threw a pleading look at Annise as her so-called friend shoved her into the room. She even caught the glint of humor in Eli's eyes as the beads swooshed closed behind her. Holly hissed at the curtain, swatting the colorful beads, then twisted onto her back and began toying with the ends.

"Loyal cat, my butt."

"Oh, she's loyal. Holly, is it?" Emma pulled out a chair at a round table and took a seat in a cushioned chair. She flapped her hand. "Come now. Take a seat. I was expecting you." She lifted her wrist to her face, swiping the screen of her Apple watch to illuminate the time. "Only about ten minutes sooner." She tapped the object as Niera cautiously took a seat across from her, not bothering to tuck herself into the table. "Fancy thing. Eli bought it for me thinking he could schmooze his way into my good graces regarding my grand-niece."

"Did it work?" Niera tilted her head toward the beads that rustled with each playful swat from Holly. "He's in your store."

Emma laughed. She reminded Niera of a jolly lady as she bounced, her curls flopping around her face until she settled.

"Eli and Sam are a sure thing. At least, last I saw."

She swiped a deck of cards from the edge of the table—tarot cards, if Niera was correct—and began to shuffle. Emma's gaze never wavered from Niera. She had the feeling the woman was picking her apart with a pair of celestial tweezers. One layer after another peeled away until she felt the undeniable vulnerability of being truly Seen. Straight-to-the-core exposed and naked before this woman.

"Hmm, I might not need these for a reading." Emma placed the shuffled deck back on the table and held out both hands, palms up. "Place your hands in mine, palms to the ceiling."

"Uh—"

Emma's grin stretched. "Are you frightened to know what's in your future?"

Niera blinked at the woman, her lips flapping soundlessly. Emma's words hit a raw chord in her soul, a quietly manifesting fear she'd held close to her heart all this time. A fear that her future would include happiness for others, but not her own.

Only two nights ago, a ghostly entity in a dream reminded her that the time to reach her quota of perfect matches was coming to a close—the day after tomorrow, to be exact—and she must complete it before a snowflake's fall.

I'm in Florida. There's definitely no snow to be had here.

Fingers twitching nervously, Niera did as the woman bid,

unfurling her fingers and resting her hands in the cradle of soft, warm skin.

Almost instantly, she saw a vision of a man embracing Emma, his energy bright and strong, wrapped in and woven with his beloved's. Instinctually, she closed her eyes and gave herself over to the vision, the recognition of the Fates weaving compliments together in a burst of gold and white light. She hadn't noted a wedding band on Emma's finger or draped on a chain around her neck.

"I see a man with you, holding you. You're not married, but…dating." The words tumbled from Niera's mouth on their own accord as her mind settled in a trance-like state that often occurred when she crossed paths with anyone possessing the characteristic signs of a Fates'-meddled destiny. "I can't gather his name, but he's of your age, quite charming, eyes like the sea."

"Philip?"

Emma's hold on her hands quivered.

Niera shook her head, casting the vision aside, but the energy thrumming between their connected hands remained strong. "I-I'm sorry. I didn't mean…"

Emma's head angled to the side, her dark gaze gauging Niera with renewed curiosity. "You saw my Philip?"

Niera shrugged, pursing her lips.

Softness brushed her elbow. She glanced down to find Holly nuzzling the side of her head against her arm, the fur tickling her skin and the small animal's quiet purr soothing the rift in her conscience.

"I'm not sure who I saw, but the man is someone who is bound to you, elementally. Fated to have you."

Emma's eyes widened and a soft gasp fled her lips. "You're capable of seeing interwoven patterns between people. A matchmaker."

The corners of Niera's lips curled. "Yes. It's part of my gift. I can see how all things of nature are woven together through their energy lines, if I choose. But the strongest visions involve people, since their life essences are usually brimming with light."

"And yet, you give the gift of love to strangers while you, yourself, remain alone. But not for long." Emma lifted her hand, cutting Niera's rebuttal off before it reached her tongue. "When you have your visions, you inadvertently open yourself up, too. And I don't see solitude in your future. I see struggle, but happiness." Her dark eyes narrowed further and she tapped a finger on the tabletop. "You have an aversion to ocean water."

"Unfortunately. I'm a fae of forests and trees. Being so near the ocean depletes my energy."

"And you came to Cat's Paw Cove to help your friend, regardless of the consequences to yourself. Ahh"—she wagged that finger at Niera, her eyes widening, an impish smile crossing her mouth—"it wasn't always so, and it shan't always be."

"I don't understand. I've had an aversion to salt water—"

"Due to a misunderstanding, yes?" Her smile grew and her face brightened with knowing. "But something plagues you and your hope of happiness. Time is running out. You'll face a choice. A life-altering decision in the near future. Once you come to the crossroads, choose wisely. Listen to your heart, not the voice in your head manipulated by this magic that imprisons you."

Nodding slowly, doubtful of the woman's prediction, Niera went along with the reading. Some of it hit raw truth, but Emma's advice remained utterly vague and convoluted, like that of most psychics. Give enough to hook a customer into believing, and play with words to satisfy curiosity.

But that truth of time and plagues...

Emma patted her hand.

"Eli!" The older woman called, her high-pitched voice ringing through the room. A moment later, the handsome man from the storefront poked his head through the beaded curtains and smiled. "Please put together a care package for my friend here. Include fire agate, desert rose, and three pouches of the purifying bath mixture. No charge today."

Niera gasped. "But—"

"I'm on it," Eli said, dropping the beads to sway until they came to rest.

Holly hopped onto her lap, brushing her tail across Niera's face before curling up in a contented ball.

"Emma—"

"I insist. Who knows"—she rose to her feet, black eyes glittering with excitement—"it might actually work."

Niera lifted Holly's light, furry body to her chest and rolled out of her chair, close on Emma's heels as they headed toward the curtain.

"I'm not sure I get what these things can do for me."

"You're a woodland fae, yes?" When Niera nodded, Emma laughed. "Surely you understand crystal magic. And the purification bath is to counter this"—she waved a hand up and down Neira's body—"cloud hovering around you."

"Cloud?"

"Dear, the curse. Or what will soon become a curse. I saw a snowflake, but its significance baffles me. Whatever task you have to fulfill is somehow linked to a snowflake."

Maybe the prophetic dream wasn't completely pointed at Cat's Paw Cove. Florida didn't get snow.

Did it?

The ominous chill that trickled through her veins begged to differ.

Either her silence or her expression gave something away as Emma gathered the beaded curtain in a soothing clickety-clack and urged her from the room.

"Sometimes visions aren't as literal as they seem, dear. Although, these parts have seen a flurry or two, if the timing is *just* right."

CHAPTER THREE

"I'll go hunt down a spot," Brayden said, separating from Alistair and Danny before either could protest. Their friend, folding chairs in hand, crossed the crowd-dense Sherwood Boulevard toward Wilshire Park, where hopefully they'd get a few good seats to see the parade from.

The sun had barely set, the sky spattered with fiery orange and neon pink through lacey clouds, but spectators lined the streets along the parade route. With the main roads blocked off in preparation for the caravan of brightly-lit floats, vendors strolled up and down, selling blinking accessories and balloons, while many local food spots offered snacks to those waiting for the show to begin. Kids played chase while kittens and cats—both those troublesome Sherwoods and the normal domestic type—swiped at the vendors for scraps or tumbled along the street between the patter of children's feet.

The laughter and elation that suffused the air brought a smile to Alistair's mouth. The muted scent of the ocean twined through the richer aromas of food. Christmastime in Cat's Paw Cove had to be one of the most magical times of the year. The town boasted plenty of magic on a daily basis, but this was different. A warm, cozy magic that opened his mind to possibilities and the dangerous illusion of granted wishes.

"There's Annie. Come on. I told her we'd meet her at Pie in the Sky," Danny said, giving his stomach a pat. "I'm starved."

"Definitely up for a few slices," Alistair agreed, letting his friend lead the way through the thickening throng.

The trip along the sidewalk to the storefront three doors down was as treacherous as a dive during a hurricane. He got smacked in the back with a beach chair, tripped by two squalling cats, and was nearly run over by a pack of children.

When he finally made it through that storm, he stumbled around a group of teens and barely caught himself against the wall of the pizza joint before mowing down a customer. Said customer splayed a hand on his chest, steadying him.

A jolt of heat poured through his skin, spread down his legs, and rattled his brain enough for his vision to fade. A few blinks later, he found himself staring down into an incredible set of warm honeyed eyes.

"I-I'm terribly…" His tongue dried in his mouth, leaving his voice scratchy and thick. "Sorry."

The woman grinned, a sweep of red crossing her cheeks as she lowered her head. Her hand slipped away, leaving an unforgiving ache in its absence.

"Just returning the favor from earlier," she said, her voice melodic and sensual. He'd never heard such an appealing sound in his life. Then again, he hadn't paid attention before. But there was something about this woman… "I should get inside."

"Let me get the door for you. I'm heading that way

myself," Alistair offered, catching the door as it swung closed after a group left the packed joint.

The woman slipped past him into the pizzeria, her fingers tying and untying at her waist. Nerves? He smiled to himself, stealing a few seconds to look her over. Petite, delicate even, that mane of shining mahogany hair tied up in a ponytail that fell midway down her back. Even in the crowded pizza joint, she moved with a fluid and captivating grace. Twist here, sidle there, until she stopped.

Right beside Annie and Danny.

Danny waved him over, but his feet anchored him to the tiled floor. The two women chatted, their voices washed out by the loud clings and clatters and cross conversations taking place in the small eatery.

"Dude! Come on!"

Danny's bellow shocked him out of the trance, the wonder, and he crossed the small distance to join his friend. Annie draped an arm over her friend's narrow shoulders, her smile blinding as she looked at him.

"You met my dearest friend, Niera, I hear." She giggled. "Niera, this is Alistair, one of Danny's surf coach buddies and a close friend."

"To finally have a name with a face," Niera said, holding out her hand. "Pleasure to meet you."

Alistair grasped her hand. Judging by the quirk of Danny's brow and the curious glance he shared with Annie, maybe too eagerly.

"Same to you." He might have held her warm hand longer than appropriate, but she didn't seem in any hurry to pull away. In fact, the longer he stared at her, the darker her eyes grew as her pupils expanded and the rose along the delicate curve of her cheeks deepened. A heat unlike any the sun provided or the sea in the dead of summer enticed poured from his fingers up his forearm, and further still, spreading like thick syrup through his veins.

It infused life he never realized he lacked. The rush of energy lingered, swelled, until all he could think about was bringing the woman closer to see if all these strange things were a gift. From her.

A throat cleared.

Niera jerked her hand from his and shuffled back a step, her eyelids fluttering. She shook her head, rubbed the back of her neck, and her lips tilted in a smile that lacked conviction. She hitched a thumb toward the bathroom at the back of the pizzeria.

"Um, I'll be right back." Casting Alistair a shaded glance, she twisted and melted into the dense crowd.

Danny snickered, punching his shoulder. "Wow, you really *are* terrible with the ladies."

He would have scowled had Annie's reaction not captured his attention. A worried crease marred her forehead and her bottom lip suffered the brunt of her concern at the edge of her white teeth.

"I've never seen her react like that before," she muttered. She patted Danny's arm. "Take care of ordering?"

She went after her friend before Danny could open his mouth. His friend shrugged and smiled.

"Well, I'm not sure what to make of that first impression."

Alistair groaned, raking a hand roughly through his hair. "Second impression, and I screwed that up."

With a friendly clap on the arm, Danny pulled him along in the line. "Dude, I don't think you screwed anything up. I mean, sparks might as well have blasted from the two of you."

"Yeah. 'Course they should have. The chick ran off." Not

even his attempt to simplify this otherwise complex circumstance eased the burden of such a strange meeting. "So much for sparks, unless you count the ones her sneakers made as she bolted."

Despite the awkward encounter, Alistair found himself watching for the two women to emerge from the bathroom. The unnerving rhythm his heart danced and that relentless flutter in his stomach mocked the tiny burst of excitement he refused to nurture.

No.

He couldn't.

Two more nights until the full moon.

Two more nights until, if all went well and those adorable, menacing kittens kept to themselves, he'd have part of himself back after all these years. The part that defined who he was and who he was meant to be.

But as his gaze lingered on the bathroom door and Danny rambled on beside him, a quiet voiced whispered in a far corner of his mind. A voice that chanted with more fervor when Annie emerged from the bathroom, Niera hooked on her arm.

The beautiful woman seemed to want to avoid noticing him at all costs, looking every way but his.

He may not need to worry about the Sherwood cats this time around.

A flush of heat slithered up the back of his neck, and that unusual burn in his fingers stoked with renewed heat.

No.

This time, forget the Sherwood cats. He'd have to be wary of a stunning stranger trekking through Cat's Paw Cove with warmed honey eyes and thick mahogany hair he ached to touch. A woman with a delicate face that reminded him of a faery and an airy glide to her step that entranced him.

If he held any hope of returning to the ocean's depths, he had to stay focused.

Determination will win this. She doesn't like you anyway.

Yes! He could make himself believe that. Easy enough.

"Think two large pies'll be enough?" Danny asked. Alistair jerked his head up as his friend's question tugged him from his thoughts. He hadn't realized the line moved so fast.

"Three to be on the safe side. You know Bray's appetite. He'll devour a pie himself."

"Good point." To the cashier, he said, "Three large pies. One cheese, one meat lovers, and one deluxe."

Annie slipped between Alistair and Danny, tossing a wink his way.

Niera kept a step behind them, hands tucked deep in the pockets of her jeans, her jacket pulled tight around her hunched shoulders as she obviously tried to make herself disappear.

She doesn't like you, Al. All the easier moving forward. Steer clear of the cats, avoid a portal, get to the ocean, and all these failed attempts will finally be worth it.

"Hey, Danny. I'm gonna head over to the park. See if I can't find where Bray set up. You good with the pies?" Alistair asked, leaning into his friend to be heard over the increasingly wild chatter. Annie frowned, her eyes darting to Niera. Alistair threw on his best smile. "Gotta make sure we have enough seats."

Annie said, "But—"

"It's fine, doll. I can handle a parade crowd and still keep those pies balanced on my head." Danny waved Alistair away. "Go ahead. See you in a few. Oh! Grab a few six-packs on the way over, will you?"

"On it." Alistair ignored the deepening furrow in Annie's brow and headed to the door. He snapped a quick grin at

Niera with an even quicker, "Later," and rushed to put as much distance between himself and the cause of his twisting stomach and pounding heart as he could.

He wasn't expecting guilt to ride his heels as he wove through the parade crowd. The potent mix of confusion, hurt, disappointment, and indifference he'd caught on her face refused to release him.

That quiet little voice in the back of his head chortled.

You can't run forever.

CHAPTER FOUR

 f Annise hadn't packed the crystals in her pocket and forced her to take a cleansing bath before leaving her small condo, Niera would have pulled the *I'm not feeling well* card and been done with the night. She was never one for crowds, especially this shoulder-to-shoulder turnout, and it didn't make her already unsettled spirit feel any better. Her glamour worked overtime to hide the points of her ears and the sharper contours of her face, as well as mute the brightness of her eyes. Annise assured her several types that paranormal and mystical creatures resided in Cat's Paw Cove. The admission didn't comfort Niera.

All this effort to counter the effects of the ocean only pushed harder at her barriers. She was shrouded in the promise of a curse in the next day or two, and she was helpless to stop it.

Unless…

Plucking at the warm cheese on her pizza, she scanned the immediate area once more, waiting to see Alistair appear. It'd been twenty minutes since they arrived at Wilshire Park. She'd learned more about Danny's friend's hot-rod than she could process. Made it halfway through a slice of pizza when she wasn't trying to wash away the effects of the ocean with a beer.

And still no Alistair.

Niera forced herself to eat a dainty bite of pizza beneath the hard scrutiny of Annise's watchful gaze.

You're here for her. Not for some stranger. You'll be leaving to return to the forest. No point wasting time.

Besides, the guy didn't seem too impressed with her. Everything that had knocked her for a surprise retracted when Alistair bid them farewell with barely a word or a glance at Niera.

Shaking off the disappointment—*so foolish to feel disappointment over someone I don't know*—she resumed her analysis of what was between Annise and Danny. She'd noticed the faint thrum of woven energy almost instantly upon Danny's approach at the pizzeria. There was certainly no mistaking that initial bond. As time went on, that energy wove tighter and tighter, falling into place with the comfort her friend exuded in Danny's presence.

Annise's intuition had been correct. The two were an enviously compatible couple. A perfect, complimenting match.

The way Danny doted on her friend left nothing to doubt.

Annise wiped her fingers on a paper napkin and cleared her throat. "Bray, did Al tell you where he was going? The parade is about to start."

Danny's friend took a swig from his beer can and shrugged. "Got me, sister. He dropped off the beers and disappeared. Thought maybe he was relieving himself."

A low beat of music cut through the crowd. The streetlights dimmed and the snowflake decorations attached to the poles lit up with a flickering silvery-blue glow. A roar of excitement, applause, hoots, and whistles filled the park, making Niera cringe. Her ears rang as the cheering toned down to a tolerable level.

Annise squeezed her knee and bounced in her lawn chair. "It's starting! Oh, you're going to love this!"

Niera forced her lips to curl into a semblance of a smile, but struggled to keep it in place.

"I'm sure I will."

If the blasted stranger would leave my thoughts alone.

What was it about Alistair that hooked her curiosity, her concern, and refused to let go? He was handsome, with his ash-blond hair ruffled by the breeze and his cross between beach and prep school attire. The man pulled off khaki pants, a white sweater with a plaid collared shirt, and deep brown loafers like a dream.

She mentally smacked herself.

So not my type.

She almost laughed. She didn't *have* a type. Who was she fooling?

"Bray, stop hoarding the beers. Pass a few this way," Annise said. Her enthusiasm over the parade, along with the natural pixie magic that had a tendency to rub off on everyone around her, infused Niera with a tinge of giddiness. Maybe that's what she needed. A bit of magic in her life. Magic that was not her own.

"Beers for the boss!"

Bray dug out a few cans and handed them to Niera, one-by-one. His dark gaze never left her, his expression openly contemplative. Inquisitive and probing as it was, his curiosity didn't bother her as she expected. Maybe because there was something truly honest about the way he tried to silently pick her apart.

He cracked open the last can before handing it to her, his

shaggy hair rippling across his forehead. "A drink can make all the difference between spectating and having fun." He whipped up his own can and tapped hers. "Cheers!"

Niera happily took a swig, face pinched, breath held, as she gulped the cold brew. Fizzy and bitter, the drink went down smooth and far quicker than she planned.

"Look at your friend go!" Bray raised his beer to Niera as she finished half the can, wiped her mouth with the back of her sleeve, and grinned. "Girl can hold her beer."

"We'll see about that," Niera countered. A giggle bubbled up from her belly and ended in a tiny burp. She smacked a hand over her mouth, darting a look between Annise and the others. "Oh, gods."

Annise folded over and laughed so hard her face turned red. "Finally!" She crashed her beer can into Niera's, liquid splashing over the opening. "Let's have some fun!"

As if waiting for the magic word, a tri-colored tail swayed between their chairs, followed by a rumbling purr as Holly appeared. Niera snickered, scooping up the cat to settle her on her lap.

"You were supposed to stay at Annise's place," she chided. The cat meowed, a pleased look in her green eyes and upturned mouth. Holly turned around and around, gently pawing at Niera's thighs before finding a comfortable position and plopping down in a ball of fur, tail flicking languidly. "Guess there's no setting rules for you, huh?"

Bray nudged her arm. "The Sherwoods are their own cats. There's no telling them nothing."

At last, Niera's muscles relaxed and warmed enough for her to lounge back in her chair and stroke Holly's soft head as the first lights of the parade caravan appeared down the street. Bubbles in place of snow gleamed in the flashing array of rainbow colors.

Niera stilled.

Snow. Snowflakes.

The prophecy.

She reached over to Annise and grabbed her attention with a pinch on her arm.

"Confirmation of the reason I came here," Niera said cryptically, cutting her gaze to Danny's back. The man had twisted around to view the parade. "You were right."

Annise's eyes widened and the smile she thought could get no wider, no brighter, became blinding. "Really?"

Niera nodded, turning a thumb to the sky. "Yep. Pretty strong connection, my friend."

"Mystical—"

"Ah, let's leave the nickname behind."

Annise nodded. She twisted her chair around and moved it closer to Danny's. Niera grinned as Annise rested her head on Danny's shoulder, earning a lingering kiss to her hair.

Ah, yes. Those two certainly had something strong linking them. The tangled web of Fates couldn't keep them apart.

And all before any sign of a snowflake.

Niera sipped her beer, ignoring the sour taste to enjoy the warmth that suffused her body, and scratched her humming kitty as the caravan drew closer. The spirit of the holidays, of Christmas, bloomed all around her. For the first time in years, she thought she might actually take the opportunity to enjoy it.

After all, the twisted, elusive prophecy implied a match would be made before the first snowflake fell.

With the dazzling speckles of light from the stars and the lustrous white moon overhead, there was no chance of snow tonight. That dark, slithering entity in the shadows of her mind was nothing more than the anxiety of the last day.

Another sip of beer.

Another stroke of Holly's head.

Another love match confirmed.

She'd played the game of Fates and won.

Then why did dread tug at the pit of her stomach like an anchor threatening to pull her to the bottom of a black abyss?

Her momentary ease shifted to something dire. An urgency that caused the crowd and the caravan to fade from sight.

Holly nudged her hand, licked her palm with a rough tongue, and nuzzled her head against Niera's belly.

"Annise was one-hundred. One-hundred matches in thirty years," she mused, her low voice drowned out by the noise of the happy crowd. "I didn't make a mistake. I *know* I didn't make a mistake."

By the gods and the fickle Fates, what was she missing?

As if sensing her discord, Holly hooked the nails from one paw into Niera's jacket and tugged. Before Niera could stop her, the cat snatched the rope cinching the small pouch of crystals and yanked the bag from her pocket with her sharp teeth.

"Hey!"

Holly leaped to the ground and trotted off, tail high, head tipped skyward, proud of her pickpocketing skills. Niera dropped her can beside her chair and lunged after the blasted cat, ignoring the sudden crash of weakness that consumed her. Darn, those crystals really were doing a fantastic job of limiting her aversion to the sea, but the rebound effect of having them snatched from her unsuspecting self left something to be desired.

No one tried to stop her as she wound through the dense crowd, keeping Holly's prancing body in sight.

"Oh, you sneaky little thing. You just wait…"

Her stomach churned, threatened to lurch.

"*Ugh.*" Swallowing back bile, she ducked her head and pushed forward. "No milk for you, bad cat."

"That's okay. I don't like milk anyhow."

Niera halted, gaze narrowing on the four-legged thief weaving between spectators' legs. That voice. It sounded inside her head. An airy, soothing voice that curled inside her mind, unhindered by the ruckus of paradegoers.

Impossible.

Holly glanced at her, a knowing gleam in her cat eyes. She gave the velvet bag a playful shake, swished her tail, and resumed her leisurely trot.

"Come on, Niera. Catch me...if you can."

CHAPTER FIVE

Alistair cracked open his third beer and took a pull, all the while letting himself become entranced in the lulling surf and the sparkle of the swollen moonlight on the dark surface. His skin prickled on his legs, a mixture of drying salt water, flaking sand, and his true form begging to come out. He'd long ago learned to ignore the ache and burn of scales refused a release. Going into the water used to be sheer torture, but the more time he spent immersed in the waves, the easier the unnatural resistance became.

Still, it never completely disappeared.

As the pull of the approaching full moon urged his body to embrace a form he'd been so long without, a few beers seemed to be the only ease for his nagging torment.

Another guzzle.

He barely tasted the delightful mixture of hops and barley over the flavor of the sea that coated his tongue.

"My time has come. How much longer do you think to punish me?"

Punish.

He chuckled with another tip of his beer can.

All this time, he thought the spell preventing him from returning to his home under the water was punishment. Then, that beautiful little friend of Annie's had to traipse into town and fill his head with thoughts. Thoughts he really couldn't, shouldn't, entertain.

He'd kept all his past relationships short, dull, for this very reason.

He had no place in Cat's Paw Cove to invite the idea of a long-standing relationship.

The little tidbits of information Danny shared before they headed to Pie in the Sky to meet Annie's close friend—now he knew who she was—made him understand she had no desire to remain in the town, either.

Niera *hated* the *ocean*. His home. The only place he ever felt comfortable.

"Would never work out," he mumbled into his beer, washing away his regret with another cool drink.

No matter how much he drank, though, no volume of beer seemed to douse the attraction he felt for Niera. He resisted recognizing how deeply he wanted to get to know her. Maybe he could change her mind about the ocean. Maybe he could make her see the beauty of the vast waters, all the treasures it held.

And when he cradled her hand in his…

Gods of the sea, what was that…connection?

Niera had felt it, too. He'd bet his chance to return to the ocean she felt the zing-pull-snap of something falling into place.

He was about to finish his beer when a familiar low-frequency vibration touched him. The sound made the hairs on his arms stand up and the tortured scales beneath his skin fight more powerfully for freedom. What always came as a prickle turned into the sensation of serrated teeth pressed into his skin.

"Damn it, no."

Alistair jumped to his feet and twisted.

A proud-looking Sherwood cat pranced toward him, its calico coat ruffling in the breeze. Something dark dangled from its mouth, but those eyes latched onto his, a mischievous glint in the silvery-green glow.

That glint had nothing to do with the moonlight and *everything* to do with botching his latest chance to return home.

He scowled. "Away with you. You won't get in my way this time."

The cat growled, lowering to its haunches, the fur along its spine bristling.

It lunged.

Alistair stumbled back, avoiding its antagonizing pounce. It landed a foot away, locked eyes with Alistair, and casually dropped the bag it carried on the sand.

"Meow."

Alistair slowly crouched, not trusting the cat as he picked up the velvet bag and weighed it in his palm. A few things jostled inside, but whatever they were weighed little. Energy seeped through the material, something that battled the very makeup of his genetic core.

"What is this?" He loosened the knot.

The cat swatted the bag from his palm before he could open it. It plopped to the sand.

"What? You dropped it at my feet. What do you want me to do, leave it?" With a groan, he gathered the bag again, this time protecting it in his fist. It obviously belonged to someone, and whatever was inside likely held magically imbued importance to its owner. "You stole this from someone—"

"Holly!"

Alistair's shoulders stiffened. *That voice.*

Actually, it was more like a screech, but he'd recognize that lilting sing-song voice anywhere, even with the angry hitch.

"Oh, you bad, bad cat!"

Slowly, he twisted, still on his haunches, and tipped his head to pinpoint the source of that scolding voice. A flush of heat battled the wariness within him as he caught sight of Niera struggling across the sand, an arm wrapped around her midsection. His gaze roved over her small form, the corner of his mouth quirking upward when he caught a glimpse of the sneakers on her feet.

Definitely not a beach familiar.

The cat slinked around his legs as he twisted his beer can into the sand to keep it upright and straightened, dangling the bag from his pinched fingers. "I take it this is yours?"

Panting, Niera hobbled a few more steps, then braced her hands on her knees. The cat scampered toward Niera, winding its sinuous body between her legs, and earned a scowl from the breathless woman.

"What…on this…gods-forsaken Earth…"

Alistair hurried to her side when he noted how pale her upturned face appeared. It certainly wasn't a trick of the moonlight, because beneath that pallor, he caught the distinct hue of green he would see on someone about to be sick. Maybe the moon *was* playing tricks, because her cheeks appeared sharper than he remembered, her eyes slanted a bit more. They glowed as if candles were lit behind them.

And her ears. Tapered points stretched up from the normal curve of the shell, quivering like an unstable hologram before fading.

Shaking off his confusion, he motioned to the sand.

"Hey, sit down. Catch your breath." He tentatively placed an arm around her waist, ignoring the potent tingle that erupted along his skin, and lowered her to the ground. "Head between your knees."

"My…bag…"

He handed her the small pouch. She clutched it to her chest, rocking slowly, eyes closed, like the bag banished all negativity. After a moment, she interlocked her arms across her bent knees and rested her forehead on them. As her hair fell over her head, he once again caught a glimpse of a shimmering tapered ear that vanished just as quickly.

Alistair narrowed his gaze on the cat. Devious little creature. The cat smiled back, showing off needle-like fangs. Pride poured off its furry little body and, when it sat, it puffed out its chest. The blotchy mask of black across its face—a feature unique to the Sherwood cats—enhanced the glow of its luminous eyes. Eerily knowing eyes.

"Why'd you take that from her?" he asked the cat. He'd not realized he was stroking Niera's back until her spine shifted beneath his palm. She turned her head to look at him, strands of rich hair cutting across her face. He took in the features of her face, but whatever tricks of light the moon had cast over her had vanished. She was just as he remembered, and that memory was a tattoo in his head.

"You're talking to a cat like she's going to talk back," she said. He was glad to see the sheen of green under her skin replaced by a blush of rose, though her eyes remained slightly unfocused. She rolled the contents of the small purse around, the items scraping together inside. "Thanks for getting them back. Don't know what got into her."

"She's a Sherwood, that's all the reason she needs."

"I'm not sure I understand." Niera sucked in a controlled

breath, released it, and lifted her head. "Not sure I understand much about this town."

"Annie filled you in on the cats, right?" When one of Niera's gently sloped brows lifted, he shrugged. "Your friend. We call her Annie."

"I already figured that out, thanks. All she said was they're not normal cats. I'm curious, though. This town is overrun by them."

"Are you feeling better? You looked like you were going to be sick."

Niera rubbed the back of her neck, turning her head to stare at the sand. The cat stood up, stretched its hind legs, and meowed.

"I caught you, now go on," Niera said, scratching the cat's ears before the calico trotted off.

Alistair stared at the back of her head—oh, what he'd give to comb his fingers through her hair, just once—trying to make sense of the complicated woman. What was it about her that made him forget, even for a moment, his goal of returning home? What was it about her that made it so easy to want to stay land-bound? What was it about this one woman that plagued his every thought, even when he tried to cast her away?

At last, Niera gave him her focused attention. Despite the faint tremors that shook her arms, she appeared as she had in the pizzeria.

Except...

Alistair motioned to his face with his finger. "Umm, your face..."

Her eyes widened. She leaned away from him, mouth open in shock. "Excuse me? What about my face?"

He gave himself a mental slap for blurting out something that sounded so ridiculous and insulting. Throwing his hands up in surrender, he shook his head and quickly said, "No, no, it's not like that. Nothing is wrong with your face. You're… beautiful. Without the glamour."

She certainly was.

Now he understood why her movements, her voice, even her presence, reminded him of a faery.

The glamour surrounding her trickled away, revealing those strange, hologram-like pointed ears that shimmered in and out of focus until they solidified. The contours of her face sharpened, her brows arched at a steeper slope, her eyes slanted.

As if the magic she cloaked her true self in muted whatever was happening between them, something else lifted like storm clouds after a torrential rain.

That tingle and burn that nudged him since their first encounter came dangerously close to exploding.

He fisted his fingers in the cool sand to keep from grabbing her head and pulling her in for a kiss, because if the sea gods only knew how tempting her glamour-free mouth was, they'd curse him to the waters to keep them apart and never let him walk the Earth again.

He almost leaned into her. Almost made a complete and utter fool of himself.

Chasing her off might be the best thing for her. And yourself.

Niera turned her face away, but he quickly caught her chin and lifted her gaze to his. He watched the magic of her glamour try to slide back into place, the fuzzy edges of her appearance shift and melt, but it failed to hold.

"Stop. Please. Don't hide yourself." He laughed, and shook his head. "I'm not the best with words when caught off guard. And you definitely surprised me"—he straightened his shoulders when her lips parted to speak—"in a very good way."

Her delicate brows pinched over the bridge of her nose. "My glamour's in place."

He shook his head. "No. I can see the real you just fine."

Her muscles tensed and her fingers curled tightly around the pouch. "I-I don't understand. I know it's in place. I can feel it. You shouldn't be able to see…" Her eyes widened as she let out a quiet gasp. "You have magic!"

It was his turn to gape. "I'm sorry?"

She poked a finger at his chest. "*You* have *magic.*"

"Uh…" Lost for words—what was he supposed to say, yes?—he cleared a non-existent knot from his throat and motioned down the beach. "Okay. Would you like to move closer to the water—"

"No!"

Her snapped answer and the sharp stab of fear in her eyes niggled at the back of his mind. She didn't merely dislike the ocean. She *feared* it. The cold, toxic essence that often accompanied fear of any kind made its way to his mouth, filling it with a bitter taste that urged him to spit. He kept his wits about him and motioned to the velvet bag.

"That's protecting you, isn't it." A statement, because pieces of Niera's intricate puzzle were starting to fall into place. "Why did you come to Cat's Paw Cove if you knew the effects of being here? I'm sure Annie would've met you elsewhere if she realized how much you fear the ocean."

"I don't *fear* the ocean." The remark was brittle and defensive, the air electric around her. After a few seconds of surf-filled noise mixed with the distant parade music and the occasional squawk of a seagull, she groaned and dropped her chin on her interlocked arms. "Fine. The ocean and I have a long-standing vendetta. It doesn't like me and the feelings are reciprocated. I'll take my mountain forests over the water any day."

"Ah, not of the water family, are you."

"Woodland." She cast him a narrow-eyed gaze, scrutinizing him for a long, strangely comfortable moment. "What do you know about the sea fae?"

If she only knew.

The loss of his fins was just the start. His animosity towards the foul beings fueled his desire to return to the waters.

His silence must have given something away. Either that, or he failed to hide his disgust at her mention of his nemesis. Niera lifted her head and eyed him, an adorable crease forming over her left brow. She stretched out her legs and cringed, making quick work of removing her shoes.

"That cat is something else," she muttered, knocking sand from her sneakers. "Got me all the way here without realizing it."

"They're good at that."

"Seems they're good at mischief. Why is that? What makes them different?"

"Well, as the story goes, the Guinevere"—he pointed to the dark silhouette of the Shipwreck Museum and the ongoing restoration project of the original ship—"wrecked a short distance off the coast. There were kittens on board from Sherwood Forest in England."

Her brows shot up. "You mean Robin Hood's Sherwood Forest?"

Alistair grinned, reclining on his hands. "One and the same."

"And they survived a shipwreck?"

"They did, as did many of the passengers. The original

founders of Cat's Paw Cove. As you can guess, many of the cats, like the townspeople, are descendants of the survivors."

"What makes them special? And how do you know these Sherwood cats from any other cat?"

Her genuine interest in the history of the town, and the fact she wasn't running away from the water, were a relief.

"Their masks." Alistair crossed his ankles and drank in the sound of the lulling sea before launching his excitement into a different dimension by looking at Niera. Even confused, the woman—*fae*—was stunning. "All descendants of Sherwood cats have this mask around their eyes. Similar to what Hollywood depicts Robin Hood wearing. The little purse-snatcher who brought you here?" He snickered. "A Sherwood cat."

"Because of the mask."

Alistair leaned closer. "Because the Sherwoods are rumored to possess magical abilities, depending on the cat and its lineage. What's in the purse?"

Niera lifted the small bag. "This? Crystals. Why?"

That explained the magical pulse he detected. "Would you care to share why you're carrying crystals? Wouldn't your magic suffice for whatever you need?"

She contemplated his request, shifting the hidden crystals around in the bag. Her full lips pressed together in a tight line. The silvery light of the moon cast her profile in ethereal radiance, one he found himself yearning to explore.

"I'd rather not."

The response didn't surprise him after her prolonged silence. If he were of sound mind—three beers and a gorgeous woodland fae apparently made him loose-tongued —he wouldn't have asked. The magically imbued crystals told him enough. Her magic didn't work here, or maybe it wasn't as potent. She needed the crystals for a reason, and that reason could reveal her weakness.

Any magical creature would be wise to keep their vulnerabilities close to the heart.

"And you? What's your gift?"

He shrugged. "Who says I possess a gift? Other than my love of the water and my skills surfing, I wouldn't say I possess much." He really didn't possess any gifts of magical importance on land. He caught her attempt to hide a shiver as the wind gusted off the ocean. "Cold?"

She shook her head, but her teeth chattered. She wrapped her arms around herself, fingers white.

"Okay, maybe a little."

Without hesitation, Alistair tugged off his sweater and handed it to the wide-eyed fae. She stared at the knitted piece before taking it from his hand.

"Aren't you cold?"

Alistair winked. "Not at all. I'd go for a late-night swim if I wasn't in the company of an intriguing woman who would probably reject the suggestion."

At long last, her lips curled and the softest, sweetest sound of laughter filled the air around them. Curse him if there wasn't magic in that melodious sound. Magic that left him reaching for her face and drawing her close. Magic that cast the rest of the world in silence, all for the calming lap of the gentle surf and the sharp intake of her breath before he pressed his lips to hers.

Magic.

CHAPTER SIX

One moment, a rush of relaxation came over her.

The next, a rush of burning delight when Alistair cupped her face and kissed her.

Stunned beyond motion, beyond words, thought, or meaning, she listened to what her body whispered, and kissed him back.

There was no explanation for what brewed and bubbled between them. No sensible or logical reason for the attraction that each heartbeat spent together stirred more awake.

The kiss. A forbidden gesture she couldn't refuse. A craving and hunger she couldn't understand.

His lips were warm, his kiss gentle and slow. Tension rolled along his fingers, that unspoken urge to turn this into something wild.

Neither relented, but both indulged in this delicacy.

Disappointment welled up from the edges of her spirit when Alistair ended their kiss. He drew back enough that she could focus on his face, the brush of rose over his angular cheeks, the shimmer of indigo eyes mixed with an unusual silvery tint locked on her. She heard his audible swallow, sensed his fight to keep the miniscule distance between them.

She understood.

She sensed it all the time.

One-hundred times, to be exact.

"Oh gods, no," she whispered, scrambling away from this touch, kicking up sand as she tried to put distance between them. "No."

"I-I'm sorry." Alistair's hands dropped to his sides, a look of hopelessness and confusion coming over his handsome face. Strands of ash-blond hair fluttered over his forehead. "That was…I hadn't meant…I don't know what…"

She was at a similar loss for words. Only, she knew the *what* of that kiss. She felt it the instant his lips touched hers. Felt it shoot like a molten bolt to the core of her soul as it melted her marrow and worked its way out.

Reluctant to confirm what she already suspected beyond a reasonable doubt, she sought the familiar warp and weave of the astral world. The unseen plane of energy lines and carefully laid pathways.

If she was wrong, she'd leave tonight. Cat's Paw Cove was nothing more than a trap that would lead her to the door of a cursed existence.

What if you're right? What will you do then?

Her stomach knotted.

The first of thousands of lines flickered into view, drawing her into the astral plane. She left Alistair fumbling for words, apparently not realizing she wasn't listening. One eye in the living realm, one in the astral, she sought the flickering light that spread along the link, a link that began in the center of her chest. It ran through knots and tangles, a true web of living essences and spiritual elements, twisting and turning, up and down, coiling and stretching—

Somewhere, within the dense knot of energy lines, her essence connected with a second line. A second strand.

Please, no.

She was the Mystical Matchmaker with one last match to make, and she couldn't perform her job if…if…

The combined lines jerked.

A bright explosion of golden light made her gasp.

The astral plane vanished, leaving her to stare at the source of her entwined life essence.

Alistair.

She clambered to her feet. The startled man followed suit, his obvious confusion dimming behind a mask of concern. And…shame?

"Niera, I swear—"

"I hate the ocean," she blurted, jabbing the hand with her shoes toward the endless expanse of dark water. She didn't doubt those sea fae were watching, waiting, plotting an attack against her as she stood on the edge of their territory. She'd lose. She'd suffer at their hands. She just knew it. Gods, were those heads bobbing in the surf? Or was that a game played by the moonlight? "I can't bear to be here."

"Okay, but—"

Niera threw up a hand, silencing him. "You don't get it. Your heart is in the sea. Mine is in the forest. No matter what, we could never be." Without a second thought, she hustled toward the boardwalk, pausing her escape to repeat, "We could *never* be."

"Niera, wait. Please!"

She picked up her pace, kicking sand behind her. The boardwalk was almost within reach. A few more feet. Just a few more…

"No, no, no. This isn't acceptable, Niera. You're not supposed to leave yet."

Two beads of light emerged from beneath the boardwalk. Niera slowed, squinting into the shadowy space obscured by sea grass and sloping sand dunes. Instinct screamed at her to run in the opposite direction, and she took a step to do just that.

A familiar face emerged from the shadows. The sweet, masked face of a devious little kitty.

"Holly, enough," Niera snapped, utterly aware of what she must look like to the quickly approaching Alistair. "Go away. I'm through with the games."

Holly hopped onto the top of the sand dune and paced the crumbling peak, her glowing eyes never once leaving Niera.

"Don't run away from him. I'll catch you if you do." If cats could laugh, she would've put money that the strange sound that passed through Holly's parted teeth was exactly that. A cat laugh. *"How about you ask him about his curse?"*

"What?"

Niera jerked straight, muscles growing taut. She shot a glance over her shoulder. Alistair remained a few feet away, but his gaze had moved to Holly, an unreadable expression darkening his face.

Tiny squeals brought Niera's attention back to Holly, who paused in her pacing, tail flicking back and forth. With a single paw, she swatted some sand off the dune.

"Go ahead, Niera. Ask him."

"The cat's talking to you, isn't it."

Niera twirled around, eyes wide as they landed on Alistair. The man had crept up to stand no more than a few inches away. The kindness in his eyes cooled as he continued to watch Holly.

"Sometimes they'll converse with you. Sometimes they won't. Depends on their agenda." His indigo gaze shifted to her face. "This one chooses to give me the silent treatment, but not you."

Talking. Cats.

A human who believes in talking cats.

Gods help me, this cat is *talking to me and this human is right to believe so. What have I gotten myself into by coming here?*

"Y-you hear them, too?" Niera stuttered, clutching the bag of crystals at her side. She had forgotten about Alistair's sweater until she swung her arm behind her, whipping the heavy item along for the ride. "She *understands!*"

Alistair's visible chagrin didn't calm her nerves. "I was telling you about the Sherwood cats and their uncanny ability to muster magic. Some speak to their owners, others choose a more monotonous, regular lifestyle. Some like to wreak havoc"—he leaned to the side and pinned Holly with a cold glower, earning a hiss—"and some enjoy ruining people's lives."

"We do not! I never did anything to him. All I know is what I've heard from my friends, and no one ever harmed him," Holly protested.

Niera shook her head, pressing a fist to her temple. "Stop doing that, Holly. Please."

"Ask about his curse. You'll see you're not much different."

Niera squeezed her eyes shut, willing the cat's voice to leave her alone.

Alistair's gentle hands on her shoulders suffused her with calm, drawing her out of her panic before it could suffocate her. She would have blamed it on her proximity to the ocean, had the ocean's effect on her been substantial prior to Holly's intervention.

"Your curse," she squeezed through clenched teeth. Slowly, she peeled open her eyelids and garnered the strength to meet his gaze. Resignation slackened his jaw and the chill he'd lanced Holly with melted. "What about your curse?"

"It's…complicated," he murmured.

The battle to look away flashed in his gaze, but he held steady.

"How?"

"How what? How is it complicated? Curses often are." He tilted his head, regarding her closely. "Aren't they? Cryptic messages, injustices. The cure often something just out of reach, if not unobtainable." He lowered his head to hers. She thought he'd kiss her to stave off her questions. Instead, he asked just above a whisper, "What's your curse, Niera? Last I checked, woodland fae don't have a severe aversion to the ocean."

The shock that ripped through her fueled her resistance. She broke free of his grip, punched the sweater into his chest, and bolted for the boardwalk.

The entire way back to Annise's condo, barefoot and cold, she kept a close eye on her trail. Anticipating Alistair at her heels. Waiting for a furry, four-legged, magical talking cat to trot up to her and cast a spell. The joy from the parade crowd tinkled in the distance, but did nothing to bring the Christmas spirit her way.

She had to leave.

No more delays.

After drawing a few curious glances due to her bare feet, Niera paused to tug on her sand-coated sneakers and picked up her pace to a jog until she reached her friend's condo.

Niera dug out the spare key and let herself into the empty abode. Darkness and shadows shrouded the small living space, except for a single light over the stove. She pulled her phone out of her jacket—thankfully sand-free—and punched in a driver request using her Uber app. Ah, good. She had twenty minutes to gather her meager belongings and hustle to the edge of town.

After scribbling a rushed apology and leaving it on the kitchen counter, she locked up, replaced the spare key in the planter on the stoop, and headed to the designated meeting spot.

The sooner she left all of this behind, the better. The forest called to her, begging her to return. To replenish the energy stores the ocean sapped from her spirit and the crystals couldn't completely preserve.

She reached Tabby Road, where her journey began earlier that day. The excitement from the crowd along the parade route down the road reached her ears. A pang of regret touched her chest. When she turned to face the festive trail of colors, sparkles, songs and sights, that pang erupted into a dull ache. When was the last time she enjoyed a Christmas? When was the last time she enjoyed anything for herself, period?

"Make sure the curse isn't cast, and then I'll have time for me."

The twin headlights of an approaching car rolled over her. She followed her driver's path on her app until the car pulled up beside her.

The doors clicked open and she dropped into the back seat. Her driver—Ed, per her app—smiled over his shoulder.

"Missing the grand parade in the Cove?"

"Not really a parade person."

"Shame. There's a little-known tradition at the end of the parade, right before the gala at Sherwood Manor. Supposedly, coins are hidden all over town. Anyone who finds a lucky coin can make a wish. Heard those wishes actually come true. Friend of mine found one a few years back." Ed sighed before he faced forward and asked, "Where to?"

Anywhere but here.

"Daytona International Airport, please."

"Gotcha."

Niera settled back into the plush seat, watching the parade's rainbow lights fade as Ed turned the car around and steered away from town. The poignant floral scent of an air freshener washed away whatever ocean breeze remained in her lungs. Her tension subsided, starting with her shoulders and moving to her legs.

She closed her eyes.

It's over. No more talking cats or falsely woven Fate strings. No more illusions of sea fae or debilitating weakness.

She swallowed, only to have a lump bob up in her throat.

No more Alistair.

"Headed to warmer or colder climes?" Ed asked, slowing at a red light before A1A. The light changed from red to green before he came to a complete stop, and he turned onto the highway.

Faded silver flashed before her eyes, blinding her briefly. Her body jerked, twisted, and suddenly she felt impossibly light, like she was floating in the air.

Then, she plummeted, and landed splayed on her back, staring up into a star-studded sky with a waxing moon illuminating the night.

She gasped, gulping in a breath as an ache unfurled from her feet to her head. She cringed, but the pain was gone as quickly as it came.

After a few blinks and controlled breaths, she saw a shadowy head loom over her face. It took her a few moments to realize the sound of rushing blood through her head wasn't blood at all.

It was the lazy lapping surf of the ocean.

The looming head tilted and a set of glowing green-silver eyes met hers. A small paw rested lightly on her shoulder.

"I'm sorry, Niera. But you can't leave. Not yet."

CHAPTER SEVEN

"Well, that's a shocker."

Niera listened to Annise's grumbling voice respond to the weatherman on the television, her mind wrapped and warped after the events of last night. She hugged her knees to her chest, rocking slowly on the sofa, her unusual behavior overlooked by her friend, who seemed more frustrated by the current events and weather predictions.

After two more escape attempts, each ending with her landing supine on the beach with Holly's sympathetic voice pleading that she stop, she finally gave up. Though the cat wouldn't explain how she was keeping Niera in Cat's Paw Cove, she did leave Niera with a haunting prediction that aligned with both her prophetic dream and Emma's ominous warning.

"To prevent a curse, you must break a curse. And it must be done before the first snowflake falls."

"If that isn't rhetorical," Niera muttered into her knees. At last, Annise glanced at her, the smooth skin over her brows pinched with worry.

"Hey, you don't look well. How much time did you spend

at the beach?" Mouth taut, she cast a curious look at the telling trail of sand that led from the front door to the guest bedroom. Niera sighed and shrugged. Annise suggested, "How about another purifying bath and I'll make you some tea. Later, we can keep things low-key and catch a movie at the Shakes-Purr Theater. Indoors, away from the ocean. Well, kind of."

Niera scanned the small condo, keeping her eyes peeled for Holly. The animals she communicated with in the forest didn't speak. Not like the cat that had chosen her as its plaything. She didn't appreciate being a fae ping-pong ball, bounced back to the beach from the edge of town. She hadn't checked, but by the feel of her rear, she sported one heck of a bruise on her tailbone.

"Earth to Niera." Annise plopped down on the sofa beside her and waved her hand in front of Niera's face. "You're really scaring me. This isn't like you at all."

"Maybe I need to rest today. Get some of my strength back. Why don't you go meet up with Danny? I'll be fine." She waved to the sand on the floor. "I'll clean up my crumb trail and call you if I need anything."

"But—"

"No buts." Niera forced a smile and squeezed her friend's hand. "I'll be fine. Just need a little rest is all. Besides, I'll be leaving tomorrow and need my strength."

"I wish you'd stay. Danny said Al was really concerned over the way you took off. He felt terrible about how things were left." Her friend's lips pursed. "How *were* things left?"

Niera threw up a hand. "Definitely not what you're implying. We talked and, being the fae I am, I didn't want to lead him on so I took off."

"Huh. Sure."

She shrugged. "Well, that's pretty much the nutshell

version of it. After tomorrow, all of this will become a moot point because I confirmed what you already knew about Danny. My job here is done and your job to go hang out with your boyfriend and perfect match is calling."

All troubles with Alistair forgotten, Annise bounced on the seat a time or two, then slung her arms around Niera's shoulders and hugged her tight. "You definitely are the Mystical Matchmaker!"

Niera laughed as Annise sat back. "I didn't make the match with you and Danny. You two did that yourselves."

Her smile faltered, her words repeating in her mind. Her friend jumped from the sofa and disappeared into her bedroom, rambling on about her plans for the afternoon, none of which Niera deciphered.

"Gods be darned." Niera whimpered, dropping her head on her knees. How had she missed it? How had she not realized Annise and Danny were not meant to stop her curse?

You were too excited about making the last match. Too sure of yourself. Too confident and you missed the obvious.

She'd made ninety-nine matches. Not one-hundred.

"You knew it, Niera. You knew Annise and Danny weren't a match requiring any intervention. You said it yourself: It was a *confirmation*."

She'd brought ninety-nine couples together, all *strangers* before their initial meeting. She followed the fickle Fates' energy lines, life essences, of those who were meant to be partnered. She knew the routine, the struggle, the obstacles, and, ultimately, the happy outcome.

Annise and Danny didn't count.

She needed to make one more match.

"Well, if nothing else, I'm in Florida, so I'm safe from snow."

Annise emerged from her room, hair styled and outfit

sharp. She had applied a light coat of makeup, but her radiant skin beamed beneath the powder.

"I'm going to meet Danny at Surf's Up Café on the boardwalk. Their morning classes end in fifteen minutes. If you need anything, you call me, got it?" Annise gathered up her small purse and car keys, and stepped into her shoes at the door. "And don't worry about the sand. I'll sweep it up when I get back."

"Nonsense. Go. Have fun." She pushed to her feet and shooed her friend out the door with a smile. Annise giggled, tugging a jacket over her shoulders before she left. Niera stood in the doorway, watching for any sign of a mischievous calico padding around the front stoop. Thankfully, her adopted feline friend—if she ventured so far as to call the cat such—was nowhere to be found. "I expect you home by nine."

"Don't wait up, Mom."

"You'll be grounded!"

Annise disengaged the alarm on her car and pulled open the driver's-side door. She waved over the roof. "Rest up. Gotta take you out for your last night here."

Niera watched as the pixie pulled out of the short driveway onto the quiet road before stepping back inside. She started to close the door when the sunlight reflected off something in the planter.

"What a good friend you are, leaving the spare key out for all to see." With an exasperated groan, Niera reached for the key. What her fingers met wasn't a key at all, but a disk. She lifted the gold coin, speckled with damp potting soil, and turned it over in her fingers. "What is this?"

Anyone who finds a lucky coin can make a wish.

Her Uber driver's wistful words teased her mind. Surely someone dropped this in the planter. Simple explanation. It didn't look like any currency she was familiar with, one side featuring a stylized image that resembled the paw of a cat, the other boasting an old-style ship with large masts and grand sails.

I'll ask Annise about it later.

Niera closed the door and engaged the lock. Gods only knew if these cats could open doors. After all, portaling someone seemed to be child's play for Holly. Or kitten's play.

After finding a broom and dustpan tucked in the tiny laundry closet, she began the tedious cleanup from her unexpected visits to the beach. The TV droned in the background until she finally gave in and reached for the remote. Comedy or a nature show would suit her mood far better than sullen and sad news stories.

Leaning on the broom, she angled the remote to change the channel when the weather forecast popped up on the screen. A cold front would be coming through tomorrow, dropping the temperature to a record-breaking low.

Niera's jaw sagged as she noted the weather map.

"No way."

"Be sure to get those kids outside because there's a chance of some rare flurries hitting the area as evening comes. The last time Cat's Paw Cove experienced snow on the mainland was in 2015, and only scattered flurries at that. You won't want to miss it!"

A clatter startled her. It took a moment for her to realize the broom had slipped from her hand and fallen to the floor. Hand to her chest, feeling her racing heart under her palm, she reached down to retrieve the broom.

"This trip gets better and better. Now, snow in Florida." She tipped her head to the ceiling and groaned. "What did I do to deserve this? All I ever wanted was to make others happy, not walk into a curse!"

As always, silence answered. Gods didn't heed the calls of those beneath them, and the Fates couldn't be bothered when they were too busy wrapping energy lines in knots for their own entertainment.

Niera scowled and resumed sweeping. As she piled the sand on the kitchen tiles, her eyes gravitated toward the coin on the counter. She ignored her impulse to snatch it up and cast a wish as she swept the sand onto the dustpan and dumped it in the garbage. But after she put the broom and dustpan away, the coin beckoned, challenging her to pick it up.

Cast a wish.

She scowled at the object. "You're trying to trick me and it's not going to work. I'm done playing by unfair rules."

"Cast. A. Wish. Any wish."

"Talking coins now. Lovely."

As she leaned closer to the counter, subtle energy hummed through her spirit, stoking her curiosity.

"What the heck," she murmured, turning the coin over in her hand. "Go big or go home." Closing her fingers around the coin, she squeezed her eyes shut and formed her wish in her head. She funneled all the energy she could into the coin.

"I wish...I wish to find my one-hundredth match and be done with curses by tomorrow morning."

Nothing happened. Then again, what was she expecting?

"Faery dreams and wishing wells. All a bunch of meaningless nonsense and a waste of time," she muttered, tossing the coin onto the counter and heading to the guest room.

Annise was right. A purifying bath and a hot cup of tea were what she needed. Maybe a nap.

Time to focus. To figure out a way to bring two strangers together before tomorrow night.

Stripping out of her clothes and tucking a towel around

her chest, her confidence dwindled. Stealing a quick glance in the mirror, looking over the sickly pallor of her glamourless face, the sallow shadows of her cheeks and the rings beneath her dull eyes, she grappled for that tiny frayed end of hope.

"There's a couple here that needs to find happiness. And I'll find them as soon as I get some energy back." Clutching the towel at her chest, she nodded decisively. "I *have* to."

THE WATER HAD COOLED WHEN THE DOORBELL JINGLED THE first few beats of a Christmas tune. Niera sighed and climbed out of the rejuvenating water, her arms and legs covered in goose bumps. Patting herself dry before tucking the towel around her chest, she opened the drain and padded into the living room.

The doorbell jingled its jolly tone again.

"Coming. Coming."

She hastened her steps, catching herself when she slipped on the tiles and almost lost her towel. She reached the door and fumbled to fix her towel enough to appear decent.

She pulled open the door.

And almost slammed it shut.

Alistair's eyes dipped to her cleavage, then immediately jerked up to her face. A heated blush coasted over his handsome cheeks. After a few awkward moments, he looked away while raising a white paper bag and drink carrier with two cups.

"I-I didn't realize…I'm, uh…I brought breakfast."

Niera shuffled behind the door, hiding her poorly clad body, and jutted her chin toward the kitchen. "I'm not a big breakfast person."

His blush darkened, causing her heart to pitter-patter and

her stomach to do all sorts of whirly moves. He actually looked…cute, all timid and embarrassed.

"Annie warned me, but when she said you weren't feeling well, I couldn't blow it off. Especially since part of your condition is my doing, I'm sure."

"No. But I appreciate the gesture." She glanced down at the loosening towel and clutched it more tightly. "Come on in. Just give me a few minutes to get dressed."

"'Course."

She closed the door behind Alistair, who kept his eyes averted as she sidled past him and hurried to the guest room. Tossing the towel aside, she pulled on the first thing she could find—shorts and a tank top—gathered her hair into a messy knot on top of her head, and returned to find her visitor at the kitchen counter, two egg sandwiches on plates. Alistair had placed the half-gallon of milk and a sugar bowl on the counter. He looked up at her and smiled.

"So, Annie said you don't care much for meat. I hope eggs and cheese are okay. And coffee?" He smiled uncertainly as he mentioned the beverage, that flush returning to his face. Niera waved his concern away and climbed into one of the two counter stools. "Is there anything I can get for you?"

"I think this is perfect. And, honestly, I'm famished. Coffee will certainly help."

"Oh, good." He rounded the counter and took the stool beside her. "I realized halfway here that you might prefer tea."

She pulled apart the two halves of one sandwich, grinning to herself. "Why? Because I'm fae?"

"That. Mostly." He peeled off the top of his cup and fixed his coffee with milk and sugar. "And Annie said you don't care for coffee."

"I don't, but that doesn't mean I don't drink it. I had a cup yesterday at the café." She took a small bite of her sandwich, hot deliciousness filling her mouth and squeezing out a moan of delight. Her belly rumbled. "Wow." Mouth full, she gestured to the sandwich in her hand. "That's good."

Alistair chuckled. "Point for me."

She shrugged, casting him a coy glance only to catch him watching her, a particular glow in his stunning eyes. She took another bite of the sandwich, at a loss for words.

"It's nice to see you with nothing on," he said quietly.

Niera almost choked on her food, coughing behind clenched teeth. Alistair held out his coffee, worry filling his expression as he patted her back.

"*What?*" Niera wheezed.

"That didn't come out the way I meant it to. Here." He pushed his cup into her open hand and urged her to drink, which she gladly did. Her face boiled hot with embarrassment. She couldn't bear to look at him. He'd practically seen her naked! "Niera, I meant the glamour. You're not wearing magic."

"Oh." She forced another gulp of coffee to get the remainder of her bite down her throat. "*Good.*"

Only when she had stopped coughing and was out of the woods from dying over breakfast did Alistair lower himself back on his stool. His hand remained on her back, rubbing slow circles between her shoulder blades. Niera wiped the tears from her eyes before sucking in a few deep breaths.

"I find myself fumbling a lot around you," Alistair said.

"Why?" Her voice sounded strained. She watched uncertainty overcome the confidence she recalled from their first meeting, when she'd stumbled into him and he'd steadied her.

From that instant, our lifelines crossed, burned together, and continue to coil tighter and tighter.

One of his brows quirked. "Really? Come on. Why wouldn't I? You're beautiful, poised—"

"Poised?" She stared at him, then laughed. "You *did* see me last night, right? I don't call that behavior as being anywhere near poised." Which brought up her next question. "How long did you stay at the beach? What did you see?"

"I tried to catch the cat, but she took off under the boardwalk. I started to follow you, but decided it was best to leave you be. I didn't want you to feel like I was some crazy stalker." His shoulders slouched enough to erase whatever confidence he had stored up for this visit. His gaze lowered, as did his hand from her back. "Listen. I don't know if it's me or what, but I can't help but wonder why I'm so drawn to you. You made it obvious you have no interest in anything romantic, and you hate the ocean—"

Niera raised her hand, cutting him off. "I hate the ocean because the sea fae drain my energy and my magic. I stay too long and they can render me helpless." She drew her lower lip between her teeth and hesitated before continuing. "it's not that I'm not attracted to you"—*gods above, if you only knew*—"but I can't stay here. Meanwhile, this is your home."

Alistair released an incredulous snort. "We're like some forbidden fairytale." His gaze shot up to hers. "No offense."

"None taken. But yes. It's a twisted and foul joke." She picked a seed from her roll and sighed. "Often how it goes."

"So where does all of this leave us? I mean, I know there really isn't an *us*, per se, but there's *something* here. Something I wouldn't mind exploring."

Niera lifted her sandwich to take a bite, buy herself some time to think up an answer, then decided evasion was the worst thing she could do. Proof sat next to her after last night.

I'm not entirely upset by it, either.

If she was stuck in Cat's Paw Cove until her blessed little

kitty friend released her from her invisible cage, she might as well try to enjoy it. Right?

Cast a wish.

She wanted all this stuff about curses to end. Wasn't that what she wished for?

"To prevent a curse, you must break a curse."

Slowly, she lowered her sandwich to the plate and twisted to face Alistair. He had shifted on his seat and was examining his sandwich before taking his first bite. She regarded his handsome profile, the ashen hair falling over his forehead and teasing his ears. The sharp contours of his cheeks and nose. The angle of his brow.

He didn't deny being cursed. Hadn't he said it was complicated, as curses often were?

"Cryptic messages, injustices. The cure often something just out of reach, if not unobtainable."

Her heart gave a deft thud, a rush of blood leaving her lightheaded. What if…

"Tell me about your curse, Alistair."

CHAPTER EIGHT

Bringing breakfast to Niera was intended to make up for whatever rift he'd caused the night before. His lack of self-control when he kissed her couldn't have won him points. His nerves ran on high-octane fuel all night, and sputtered all morning, the unknown looming like a storm cloud over his day.

He woke with one goal: Make things right with the enrapturing woodland fae.

He only hoped that everything else would fall into place.

Bringing up his curse certainly wasn't on his list of topics to discuss over breakfast. Not after his tongue fumbled obscene words and a timid, shy boy-creature possessed his otherwise confident mind. That's what Niera did to him. She made him nervous. Made him worry he wasn't enough, couldn't be enough, and he desperately wanted to be everything she could hope and wish for.

Gods, if only he'd gotten his hands on that Sherwood cat…

"My curse," he said slowly, abandoning his sandwich for

a thoughtful sip of coffee. "How about this: I'll tell you mine if you tell me yours?"

"What makes you think I'm cursed?"

The hitch in her voice gave away her reaction to his suggestion. Fact was, he didn't know if she was cursed, only suspected there was more to her fear of the ocean, the sea fae, and her desperate desire to keep miles between herself and a possible relationship.

Every instinct assured him she fought whatever this connection was harder than she struggled to hold onto her energy and magic because of those pesky sea fae.

Staying just out of reach. Almost unobtainable. Typical curse irony.

"I'm not, but something tells me there's a bit of dark hexing sparking your every decision since you arrived here."

A little nudge, but no outward deductions. Maybe, just maybe, she'd indulge his curiosity and help him understand why she continued to push him away when it was obvious she didn't want to.

"Okay, I'll make you a deal." He lowered his cup to the counter and faced her fully. Gods, every time he looked upon her face, his heartbeat went haywire and his skin tingled like someone held a torch near his flesh. A pleasant burn without the damage. "I'll entertain you with the details of my so-called curse, but in return, you must tell me why you're so against pursuing something with me. Even if it's a friendship."

Niera perked up. "That's easy. I'm a loner." When he tilted his head and stared at her without speaking, she sighed. "Okay, fine. I agree." She pointed a finger at him. "But you can't leave anything out."

"It's not so convoluted that I'd forget the details." A humorless chuckle escaped him. He brushed aside a wayward strand of his hair, folded his hands on the counter, and leaned on his forearms. "Believe it or not, it's pretty straightforward. I was lured by one of those malicious sea fae into a courting relationship, not realizing she was promised to another. That other was a cousin of mine, distant, but a relation. My uncle thought I was trying to sabotage a contract between his family and the female sea fae's family so my parents would gain more wealth and move up the social ladder. What he didn't know was that my father didn't need me to marry for money or social standing. He was the advisor to one of the"—he waved a hand in a nonchalant manner—"most prominent families in our city, though his position and that connection was kept quiet. The only reason I knew was because I was set to succeed him and had begun attending sessions and meetings to follow in his footsteps."

"Why would it be a secret? Your father's position?"

The corner of his mouth curled. He'd kept his true roots close to his heart. Not even Danny and Brayden—both of whom were considered "regs," Cat's Paw Cove's lingo for human—knew much about his past. When it came to Niera, his tongue loosened and the urge to spill all the details came overwhelmingly easy.

"To preserve his life, and the well-being of his family. Being an advisor to this particular person is fraught with danger. Kidnapping. Murder. Ransom. You name it. My father kept the family's financial status hidden and his position masked behind a calculated front." Alistair shrugged. "In hindsight, I suspect the female had an idea about my father's position, my inherited position, and decided to play the seductress. I had no knowledge about the pact her family had with my uncle's family, so it wasn't deliberate on my part."

"Hold on a moment." The hesitation in her voice drew his attention. She watched him with a mixture of curiosity and speculation that both warmed him from the inside-out and made him squirm in his chair. "Why am I starting to suspect you might be a sea fae yourself?"

"Close, but if I were related to the sea fae, I'd be embarrassed to admit it." He shuddered for effect, earning a smirk from the pretty fae. "Another sea-faring creature."

Niera's probing gaze burrowed deep. It felt like being picked apart in a rather pleasant way. To give her a hint, he lowered some of the walls he kept around his magical essence. It was the first time since he'd become land-bound that he let anyone within his barriers.

He didn't trust the sea fae not to send one of their spies to meddle with his life.

Niera's eyes widened, the warmed honey hues of them casting their own spell over his mind. "Merman."

He winked. "Beautiful *and* smart."

She flushed a pretty rose he couldn't keep from tracing along her cheek with his fingertips. She ducked her head, a shy gesture, but he caught the twitch of her lips before they curled up.

"That explains your love of the ocean, which is my bane."

Her silence weighed heavy, unspoken words churning in the air between them. There was something more she wasn't revealing, he was certain.

"It shouldn't be. Woodland fae, at least in my understanding and studies, hold no aversion to salt water. You're an exception, and your evident dislike for the sea fae makes me wonder what curse they settled on you."

Niera laughed and shook her head. "I see what you did. Handsome *and* smart." Her eyes glittered with anticipation. "You're correct about my disdain toward the creatures, but they have nothing to do with my looming curse."

Alistair straightened, a dark smile coming easily to his mouth. "So there *is* a curse involved."

"I don't think you were through telling me about yours."

"Quite boring, actually. My uncle conspired with outcasts from the city, the dark sea fae that swim the depths. Both families, his and the female sea fae's, had been shamed, and the only way to fix it was to cast out the one at fault. Unfortunately, they all blamed me. To ensure the bonding occurred between my cousin and the female, I was the one exiled. For good measure, they decided to take it one step further." He swung his legs, softly kicking the counter with the tip of his shoes. "Earned myself a pair of legs and no magic to change back into my scales. Here I am, an exiled merman, and my only hope of ever salvaging my reputation and regaining my place as my father's successor is to break the curse."

"And how do you suppose you break it?"

That was the tricky part.

"No one knows that a servant of my father's leaves me gold in the reefs. I go diving ever week, or that's what my friends believe. My ability to stay under water is limited to about ten minutes, fifteen max. Far longer than the average human, but it's nothing compared to what I've know most of my life. Still, it's enough time to reach the reef and retrieve my allowance, as you might call it. It's also a discreet way of communicating with my family and letting them know I'm okay, as well as learning what I need to do to break the curse."

"Which is?"

"Get my fins back. And to do that, I must find the sea fae who cast the curse. My father has sought that sea fae for years. When my uncle was implicated in some questionable activities, he offered the name of the fae to avoid a death sentence."

Niera's brows shot up. "Your people don't mess around, do they?"

Alistair scowled. "He took a shot at my mother's life. He deserved a spear through his cold heart. Last correspondence I received was that she still suffers effects from the damage of the fae's poison. It's made me all the more anxious to return home."

"If you know the name of the fae, what keeps you here?"

"Cats." His laugh was a cold, humorless guffaw. Niera made a distressed sound and slumped back on her stool. "As you probably experienced, given your reaction."

"Holly said she couldn't let me leave. Whatever she did, I can't pass beyond the outskirts of town. I tried three times last night. Each time, I ended up portaled back to the beach with a pitying cat staring down at me."

He couldn't help it. He chuckled until he laughed and shook his head, reclining on his stool and crossing his arms over his chest.

"I told you. The Sherwoods have some sort of magical powers. Some talk to you, some choose to be more unassuming, but are no less guilty of menacing behavior." He gave the counter one final tap with the toe of his sneaker and sighed. "For three nights, I can assume part of my mer features. No fins, but I can stay submerged for the duration of the full moon, starting the night before the peak and lasting through the night after the peak. The trouble comes when I try to get to the water. Those Sherwoods put up a boundary that will not let me wade into the ocean. I was planning on trying to go down A1A a bit, but after your experience, I'm wondering how far this boundary stretches."

"And it's only during the full moon?"

"Yep. I can go into the water any other time without a hitch. And it's not the sea fae keeping me out. They want me in the water so they can gnaw at my limbs and torture me. So, that's my sad tale. I can break my curse by finding the sea fae who cast the darn thing on me, but I can't reach the water during the full moon to do so." He shrugged, clearly trying to lighten his solemn mood, and flashed her a forced smile. "Your turn."

Niera picked at the seeds on her roll, tossing each extraction on the plate. After a few long moments of silence, she shifted on her stool and faced him, her hands folded in her lap as she swung her legs.

"I was always the fae who saw perfection in the connection of two people, despite the struggles to make that pairing possible. It was a gift, one I cherished, and one the Fates deemed me worthy of. I became the Mystical Matchmaker a few decades ago, but with the title came the responsibility of ensuring those I brought together were *meant* to be together. You see"—she wagged her hand between them—"I can sense a fated connection. I can see the lifelines entwine and light up. I know when two people are meant to be together because it's inarguable. My gift makes it so. The Fates thought it a gift to bestow the chore of matching one hundred couples. They warned me I had a time limit, but never told me what that limit was.

"Then, I had a dream before coming here that I had reached the end of my road. If I can't make my one-hundredth match by the time it snows, I'll be cursed to live alone, surrounded by everyone else's happiness, with no hope of being happy myself."

"But you isolate yourself?"

She lowered her head. "I've left myself no time or leeway for romantic involvement while I rush against an unseen clock. Do you know the effort it takes to get strangers to realize they're meant for each other? There were times I wanted to beat my head against the wall, but in the end, their happiness filled a deep well inside me a little more."

"You came here to play matchmaker with Annie and Danny to fulfill your deed," he realized aloud, rapping his fingers against his biceps. "Only they were already together, so you didn't have to put in much effort."

"I thought they'd be my one-hundredth. Holly believes otherwise."

"Ahh." He dropped his head back and looked up at the ceiling. "It always comes back to the cats. What happened between you and the sea fae?"

"I stole a human love interest from one and handed him to his true mate. The sea fae didn't take it well and banned me from the sea."

He lowered his head and watched her nervously playing with her nails and swinging her legs.

"So your revulsion for the ocean doesn't come from your genetic makeup, but a spell."

"A curse."

"No. A spell. A repelling spell. Nothing more. It's a smoke-and-mirror spell to makes you experience sickness and revulsion when, in fact, your body and magic aren't affected at all. I've seen it plenty." He rubbed the back of his neck and released a sharp sigh. "I should've realized it sooner. I knew it didn't make sense that the ocean stole your magic."

"You've seen it before?"

He pursed his lips, met her eyes, and nodded once. "They like to traipse around with humans and lead them to the sea. Those lucky enough not to be lured to a watery grave are those who find another human to love. Sea fae are infamous for their jealousy. They end up casting spells on the invading lover, repelling them from the ocean in hopes of luring their love back. Seldom does it ever happen. It's something the king—"

Alistair choked on his words, smacking a hand to his mouth. How on Earth did *that* slip through?

Niera's eyes narrowed, her head tipping to the side. She didn't say a word, not while she watched him, dissected his soul, and came to her own conclusion.

"Your father's boss is a king. A monarch. *That's* why you keep the position a secret."

Well, he certainly let the cat out of the bag. Hah.

"And you're next in line to be his advisor."

"You sum it up so graciously."

"Hmm."

Alistair reached for her hands, expecting her to pull away, surprised when she let him interlock a few of their fingers. "I fear there's something you're not telling me. What can I do to help you make your one-hundredth match?"

Her eyes warmed, her pupils growing by the second. Her face softened, but the sharp fae angles he was quickly coming to adore didn't disappear behind her glamour. That strange tingle she evoked started in his fingertips and coasted through his hands, up his arms, heat following steadily on its heels. The kitchen began to fade at the outer edges of his vision, that grayness spreading until all he saw was Niera. All he knew was Niera. All he wanted was Niera.

"Break your curse. Prevent mine from coming to pass," she whispered. "You're my hundredth."

He jerked, startled by her revelation. There was no way she meant to set him up with another woman. Not when this…this…spark grew between them.

"I don't understand. You know my mate?"

Slowly, she nodded, never once blinking. Never once breaking eye contact.

"Who," he whispered.

Silence stretched. Seconds ticked by. She stared at him, leaving him to itch in his skin, begging to ask again.

When he thought he'd go mad, he opened his mouth to repeat his question.

She cut him off. Stopped him in his tracks. Froze him where he sat.

All with a quiet, "Me."

CHAPTER NINE

"Tomorrow is the peak of the full moon."

Niera swallowed the rush of sickness that pummeled her stomach and threatened to relieve her of the breakfast she'd eaten hours ago.

Gods, she wished she hadn't allowed Alistair to convince her to leave her crystals at the condo.

The daytime temperatures had dropped by early evening. Gray clouds swept across the sky, darkening an already dismal day. The surf crashed to the sand a few feet away, spraying them with chilled seawater.

She squeezed her eyes shut, pressing her head against Alistair's shoulder. The motion came so naturally she hadn't tried to stop herself from finding comfort in him.

His hand cupped the side of her exposed face, protecting her from the spray. His thumb stroked along her brow, over and over, his touch lulling and relaxing.

"You know, I've come to a point in my life where I don't mind being land-bound," he said loud enough to be heard over the raucous waves. His tone held a gentleness she clung to. "If you're certain of what you see, I'd be willing to give up the ocean, my fins, and whatever else I must to stay here with you. I can't deny there's a connection. A pull that is relentless."

A rumble echoed through his chest and she bit back the urge to smile with his laughter. Since divulging the truth to him, Niera embraced the fickle Fates' matching. What she felt for the land-bound merman went beyond physical attraction. Beyond curiosity.

No.

It fell into the deeper realms of perfection, however imperfect their relationship might grow to be.

"You can't turn your back on what you're meant to do. Your duty to your city, your family."

Even as she spoke, dread tore through her. She didn't want him to leave her for the ocean depths. She was a land fae who cherished the forest. He was a creature of the water.

Oh, you fickle little Fates. Blasted silly sisters.

"If the Fates deem my place is here with you, then I'll gladly do exactly that." His fingers slipped to her hairline, rubbing over the rebellious strands that refused to stay in her messy knot. "My family's wealth will allow them to live a comfortable life through the end of their days. It won't be the first time the king has been left to choose a new advisor."

"You're willing to sacrifice everything based on my word. A stranger's word."

She tipped her head up to find him gazing down at her, his expression thoughtful and his indigo eyes full of restrained excitement.

"Tell me, Niera. Is that what you propose to your couples when you're making a match? Do you play devil's advocate with all your Fate-laced clients? In my opinion, that's not good marketing."

He had a point, if she were making a match that didn't

include herself. However, she'd seen so many of her matches ask the same question of their partners.

Can we trust a stranger at her word?

The answer always ended up being yes.

"When can you attempt to go into the sea?" Niera asked, scooting closer to Alistair. Despite the chill in the air, the man emanated enough heat to warm a small army. So unexpected from an otherwise cold-blooded creature.

She took advantage and snuggled into his side. He put his arm around her shoulders, holding her close.

"Once the sun sets. Clear skies or not, the beginning phase of the full moon starts this evening and I can try to get into the water." He rested his cheek on the top of her head. "You holding up okay?"

Despite the occasional flip of her stomach as it fought to purge whatever contents remained, she actually felt okay. Her energy, her magic, didn't feel as depleted as it had the night before.

"So far, so good."

"Let's hope that no Sherwood cats decide to take a late evening prowl on the beach."

TWO HOURS LATER, THE SKY HAD DARKENED AS NIGHT CREPT over Cat's Paw Cove. The boardwalk glowed with the illumination from restaurants and arcades, blinking Christmas lights adding a festive feel to an appropriately chilly night.

Other than leaving to grab a light dinner of sandwiches, Niera and Alistair sat together on the beach, watching the angry waves. She kept her eyes peeled for sea fae heads bobbing in the white foamy crests, and relaxed when none appeared.

Maybe her eyes had played tricks on her the night before.

"If you can get to the water, do you think your fins will appear?" Niera asked.

Alistair, one arm draped casually over his bent knee, one around her back, shrugged.

"I don't know what to expect other than being able to swim underwater like I did before the curse. Fins would hasten my ability to swim, but I'm strong either way. *If* I can make it into the water." His fingers tightened on her side. "How're you feeling? You seem to be doing much better than last night."

He was right. She'd pondered her lack of illness and energy depletion, noting that last night, she'd experienced a similar resistance to the spell while in Alistair's company. Maybe it had to do with their fated connection, or maybe with his ocean affinity.

Either way, she was grateful to experience the ocean without the threat of being sucked to a husk and left to blow away in the wind. Or leaving her stomach turned inside-out on the sand. She had never expected to find beauty in the sound of waves or the cool sand sifting between her toes.

She certainly never expected to find peace with a man of the sea like the one beside her.

"I think you do something to repel the effects of the spell."

"Or it's just me," he teased.

"Maybe." Lifting her head from his shoulder, she looked out at the roaring ocean. "You think it's time to try?"

Alistair nodded once, glancing around the beach. She searched for any cats that might keep him from breaking his curse. No signs of furry cuteness littered the shore.

"If I can get to the water, I don't expect you to wait here.

Not without your crystals if I can't offset the effects of the spell."

She became aware of the tension in his muscles as he brushed sand from the rolled-up hems of his jeans. He kissed the top of her head and stood, scattering sand in the squalling wind. The moment their connection broke, the sea fae spell seeped into her bones, unleashing a merciless attack on her gut. She clutched her midsection and squeezed her eyes closed, willing away the sickness.

"Niera. Go back to Annie's."

"What if you can't reach the water?"

She dared to lift her chin and meet his eyes. Perseverance, determination, and a stroke of worry rolled over his face.

"This is the first time in years the cats haven't come to the beach the night I try to enter the surf. I don't know why, but I'm not going to question current circumstance. However, you're growing paler by the second. You need to go."

Niera nodded, accepting Alistair's hand—and the subtle protection of a skin-to-skin connection—as he pulled her to her feet. She brushed sand from her pants and shivered, despite her warm attire.

"I want to make sure you reach the water."

Alistair grinned.

He cupped her face and drew her close, pressing a kiss to her lips. A sweet, slow, toe-curling kiss that infused heat through her blood, even as he stepped away.

"I'll be back tomorrow."

Niera hugged herself as she watched Alistair jog to the water's edge. He stopped a couple of feet back from where the surf spread over the sand before pulling back into the choppy waves. His shoulders rolled as he lifted his sweatshirt over his head and cast it aside. Lights from the boardwalk cast his muscular back in an array of enticing shadows, daring her to drool.

He tossed her a glance, then slid a bare foot closer to the water.

The faintest caress of pressure touched her calf.

She snapped her head down.

"Oh, no. You're not stopping him this time," she hissed at her feline friend.

Holly slid her body along Niera's leg, hindquarters lifting, tail high. Sparkling green eyes glowed as they gazed up at her, and that ever-present smile on the cat's mouth.

Niera shot Alistair a desperate look, but he'd turned away.

She gasped.

Ocean water churned around his ankles as he waded into the water.

"But…but…"

"Niera, you need to learn to trust me. I told you what must be done. Let him do his part so you can do yours."

Her stomach lurched, a warning that she wasn't protected by Alistair's presence any longer. She couldn't tear her gaze from his majestic form as he waded deeper and deeper, until he paused, waited, and dove into an oncoming wave.

The strangest sensation of a cord yanking her tight jolted her forward. She caught herself before she stumbled, shuffling back a step.

Alistair didn't resurface.

"Don't linger. You'll be sick until he breaks his curse and casts your spell aside. You're safest with Annise tonight. Away from where the sea fae can snatch you."

At the mention of the sea fae, she swore she caught sight of a bobbing head after a wave crested and dispersed into the water.

"You're right. But you and I will have a long talk about

portaling without consent, and parlor tricks that are unnecessary."

Holly meowed, then released a low, rumbling purr as she wove between Niera's legs. After a final glance at the ocean, Niera reached down and lifted Holly into her arms, nuzzling her cheek to the cat's.

"I really should be infuriated with you right now."

Holly made another noise, then pushed her triangular head beneath Niera's chin.

"Okay, okay. Let's go."

Casting one final look at the water, she pressed her lips together. Coolness filled a sudden void in her soul, but hope flared bright in the recesses of her mind. She could only hope he was able to break his curse before the flurries came down on Cat's Paw Cove tomorrow night.

CHAPTER TEN

$\mathcal{D}$own, down, down.

The pressure of the water as he dove welcomed him into its long-awaited embrace. The rough surf on the surface didn't reach these depths, and for that he was grateful. He may possess extraordinary strength when it came to swimming, but he lacked his full abilities while forced to remain in bipedal form.

His eyes adjusted to the dark waters more slowly than he could have wished. He was miles from his city, the underwater kingdom he strove to return to. There would be no getting there quickly, and he wasn't even sure whether his human form would grant him passage through the kingdom's magical borders. The extent of his curse had always eluded him, partly because, until tonight, he'd never had the opportunity to return.

The reef came and went, the gentle lull of the currents soothing caresses over his hard-working mortal muscles. He'd considered shedding his jeans, but decided he might need them when he returned to land.

That was never part of the plan until Niera came along.

Alistair knew he needed to follow this path, find the sea fae who created his curse, and make things right. Before he met Niera, he anticipated returning to his family and rebuilding the life he'd been working so hard to achieve before his banishment.

Now, he wanted the curse gone and Niera beside him. If that meant he lost his fins permanently, he'd gladly make the sacrifice. It was his decision, his *choice*. Not something forced on him.

He twisted in the water to peer toward the surface, but he'd descended too far to see anything. Thankfully, the sea fae remained in their underwater caverns tonight, their unnerving magic undetected in the water around him.

As he rolled in the water to continue his journey, he caught sight of something shimmering white to his left. He froze, vulnerable in these open depths, until the approaching figure became more defined.

A flood of relief struck him as he recognized Marin, one of his father's trusted servants, swimming up to meet him.

The merman hadn't changed much over the last few decades, except for the length of his white mane and a few added creases around his eyes and mouth. He drew up in front of Alistair, looked him over with large, soulful black eyes, and held up his webbed hands in a gesture of welcome. His tail swayed lazily, the ribbon-like fins rippling.

"After all this time, you come."

Alistair nodded. He opened his mouth to speak, sputtered as water poured in. He didn't choke on the water itself, his mortal body merely reacted to the invasion. On the second attempt to open his mouth in reply, something inside his body clicked in recognition.

"Yes."

The word came easily. Naturally. As if he'd never left the

sea. A little rusty, as proven by the harsh rasp on the final consonant, but clear.

"I…had trouble getting…here…before."

Marin nodded, sympathy filling his large eyes. "I have come to meet you every full moon once we understood the curse. Until tonight, I've had to resign myself to delivering the same sad news to your parents. There will be much joy when you arrive home."

Alistair flicked his hand toward his legs. "I must find the…sea fae who…cast the curse."

Marin's lips stretched in an inhuman grin. "The witch has been kept a prisoner within the palace walls, heavily guarded until your return. Come the morning, all will be feasting in celebration."

Alistair managed a smile, but his heart ached at Marin's words. How was he going to break the news to his parents that he didn't plan to stay? How was he supposed to turn his back on his duties once he regained his true form?

How could he in good conscience celebrate his return when he knew, deep in his soul, he would do all he could to go back to Niera?

He had until tomorrow evening to return to her if there was any hope of deflecting her curse.

"Alistair? You look…unhappy."

Alistair shook his head, snapping himself out of his thoughts. "There's much I need to discuss with Father. We shouldn't waste time."

Marin bowed his head. "Of course. Follow me."

THE KINGDOM BOASTED ALL ITS FAMILIAR GLORY FROM HIS memories. Gold accented every spire of every building, leading up to the magnificent turrets of the castle. Merfolk swam along, curiosity holding their attention as Marin and Alistair passed. He kept his eyes averted, not wishing to waste another moment to reach his parents.

Instead of bringing him home, Marin led him straight to the castle doors, where two guards eyed him cautiously before granting them entrance.

"Come," Marin said. Alistair did as he was bid. He had no other option. His time was not his to spend.

Marin led him through watery tunnels that glowed with bioluminescent algae and magical creatures that scurried through rippling seaweed.

"Where are we going?" Alistair finally asked.

"After your mother was poisoned, the king insisted your parents take a residential suite so he could extend his protection over them. With your future unknown, your father believed it was a wise decision. The king took in your family's staff, appointing them to positions within the castle, but I've remained by your father's side."

They swam deeper into the castle until Marin stopped before a gold door and knocked.

Alistair's breath hitched and his heart began a hard-beating rhythm in his chest.

The latch clicked and the door opened inward.

And for the first time in decades, he laid eyes on his father's familiar face and close-cropped hair and multi-hued fantail.

Blue eyes widened and his father's jaw slackened, leaving his mouth agape. The burn of human tears stung Alistair's eyes, but were stolen by the ocean water.

"Father," Alistair croaked.

"Son."

The older merman swept Alistair into his arms, pulling

him close, squeezing him with the strength of years of pain, anguish, longing, and the endless hope that he would return. Alistair embraced him with as much fervor, as much yearning, soaking in all he had lost and missed since suffering his curse.

"Who knocked on the—"

Alistair lifted his head from his father's shoulder and caught his mother's shimmery silver eyes as she stopped speaking. His father released his hold, turning to present Alistair with a shaky smile.

"Mom." Alistair kicked forward, having to fight his human body's buoyancy to stay level with his mother. The passing of years and the attempted poisoning had taken a toll. Despite the dull cape of hair, the sallow pull of skin over bony cheeks, her frail figure and limp tail, her eyes sparkled with strength. "I finally made it home."

Her chin quivered, but she swam closer, her gentle fingers stroking over his face. "My dear son. Look at you. Handsome as ever." Her gaze lowered to his legs, then met his eyes again. "You've finally returned, but you don't plan to stay."

Alistair tried to laugh off her concern, but she shook her head, capturing his face between her hands.

"I am your mother. I can see these things. You've been gone a long time and have adjusted to this alternate life." Her silvery eyes narrowed, but a faint grin touched her pale lips. "Who is she?"

"Nonsense. Our son's returned! We must celebrate, after that hexing witch breaks the curse she placed on him," his father interrupted, slinging an arm around Alistair's shoulders. "Come, come. It's time to make this right. So much time has been lost. Once we get your fins back, we'll celebrate your return."

Time. One thing he didn't have much of if he planned to help Niera.

As his father spun him toward the door, his mother's gentle hand on his wrist pulled his attention. She smiled, a sad but understanding motion, and nodded.

His mother understood his dilemma.

Convincing his father might be a curse of a different level.

After sending word to the king of his return, Alistair and his father were escorted to the punishment cells deep within the ocean's floor. The four guards brought them to a cell set away from the others. The magically reinforced iron bars contained a meek little sea fae, gray skin wrinkled beneath translucent scales. Tangles of gray hair snaked around a sunken face and milky white eyes.

The creature cackled, a bone-shuddering sound.

One of the guards knocked his gold-tipped spear against the bars. "Enough, old witch. Your time has come. You're bound by your sworn word to reverse a curse. One you placed many years ago."

She turned those eerie eyes on Alistair. "I'm aware of the curse, and I'm aware of my promise." His skin bristled as she looked him over, the colorless orbs burning a trail along his body. "Is this what you wish? To be released from one curse to suffer another?"

Alistair glowered at her. "What are you talking about?"

The sea fae flipped one hand palm up, followed languidly by the other. She mimicked a scale of balance, moving her hands together, one up, one down, and then reversed them.

"You well know that if you return to the sea, you will

leave her forever. But should you wish to return to her, perhaps keeping the curse intact—"

"You will break my son's curse, and you'll do it now!" Alistair's father bellowed. The water shuddered around them. "No more riddles, witch!"

The sea fae hissed, baring needle-like teeth. "I speak with the cursed, not with his family." Smoothing out her scowl, she returned her blind attention to Alistair. "What do you wish for?"

The crossroads. The irony of curses.

To save Niera, he had no choice but to break his curse. As the prophecy evolved, according to her, this very moment had to come to pass. He would sacrifice his fins to be with her, but he'd condemn her to a life of loneliness if he didn't break his own curse, forcing him to remain in the sea.

Instead, he would have to sacrifice his future with Niera in order to save her.

The sea fae giggled, the terrible, scratchy sound making his skin crawl.

"Decisions, decisions," she taunted. "Am I right?"

Alistair gritted his teeth, contemplating his options. He swam closer to the cell, gripping the bars to keep his body steady.

"The curse needs to be lifted, but I have one request."

The sea fae tipped her head to the side, and he got the feeling she was assessing him beyond his skin. She pulled her hands together and tapped her fingertips in a methodical wave.

"I may be willing to entertain your request."

"Let me see her. Tomorrow. Lift the curse, but I will see her one last time."

She contemplated his request, the silence ominous in the shadowy waters.

At last, she clapped, startling Alistair. "Very well!"

Alistair wondered about her excitement as she sliced open her palm with one sharp claw. Using the tip of her finger, she coiled a silver-blue ribbon of blood from the open wound. She moved quickly, like a trapped minnow, working with the trail of blood as she stirred the waters of the cell, muttering incoherently.

One second she was fluttering about, the next, she had Alistair by the neck, the ribbon of blood pushing into his nostrils, guiding down his throat, and latching onto something dark and tarry within his body.

"This may be a little uncomfortable," she whispered.

Pain, like parts of his insides were being ripped from his body, squeezed a bark from his chest. Somewhere in the rush of agony and blood in his head, he heard his father yell, felt the guards pull at his arms.

All the while, the sea fae chanted, releasing him to the guards as she fled to the back of the cell.

His legs burned and throbbed, his body jerked and twitched. He couldn't see a thing, blinded by whatever was happening to him at the hands of that deceitful creature. He kicked, writhed, and, when the pain became excruciatingly unbearable, bowed his back as a roar tore up from the bowels of his soul.

Blackness consumed him, suffocated him, dragged him to a place he feared and welcomed.

But one last thought wrenched his heart.

Niera. I'm so sorry. I failed you. I failed us.

CHAPTER ELEVEN

*N*iera paced the boardwalk, shivering beneath the heavy jacket she'd borrowed from Annise. The moon loomed, large and white behind scattered clouds, casting a bluish hue over everything touched by its light. Her pouch of crystals rolled between her fingers, tucked deep in the jacket's pocket.

"Maybe this isn't a good idea. It's apparent the saltwater isn't doing your nerves any good," Annise said. The pity in her tone firmed Niera's determination to stick this out. She wasn't giving up. She was too close.

She wanted Alistair beside her, safe and curse-free.

Holly appeared in front of her on the boardwalk, sand puffing up around her paws. She gave them a brisk shake. *"He's down the beach. One of my friends is staying with him. You must hurry."*

Niera gasped. "He's returned."

"You must go alone."

Niera spun to Annise and grabbed her shoulders. "Wait here for me. Please. I'll be right back."

"Nier—"

"Please."

Frowning, Annise nodded. Niera thanked her quietly. Holly trotted toward the ramp to the beach. Despite the cold air and her frozen appendages, Niera removed her sneakers and chased after the calico.

The evening air blew with the promise of a storm as it washed away the moonlight behind thick, gray clouds. Tangled within the briny air, she scented something different. A crisp cleanness she'd detected so many times before.

Right before a snowstorm.

She hastened her run. Holly paused a few yards away, waiting for her to catch up. The beach tapered up, sand dunes growing by the foot, saw grass sprouting in thicker chunks as she went. Rocks roughened the soft sand until she found herself stumbling over coral and rock to reach the spot where Holly perched on a dune.

"I promise you, it's Alistair. Don't be shocked."

Shocked?

Niera climbed against falling sand to the top of the dune, and peered into a dip between her dune and the next.

A creature both handsome and incredible clawed away from the water that lapped at the iridescent cape of an indigo tail. The lower body had a multitude of purple-hued scales that melted into a very muscular, very human-type waist and back, but the skin was a gray-purple shade that blended with the scales. Ash-blond hair plastered to a face with razor sharp angles and large eyes.

The hands, those claws.

Translucent membranes created webs between fingers, and fingers tapered into sharp, pointed nails.

"Alistair?"

The creature stopped clawing the sand. His head snapped

up and pupil-less eyes stared at her, filled with sorrow and regret.

"Niera."

A strained sound escaped her throat as she slid down the dune and scrambled to his side. Alistair pushed himself over and sat upright, the bottom of his tail flapping hard against the sand and rocks.

She grabbed his hand and cupped his cheek, ignoring the difference between her skin and the slick, leathery texture of the merman before her. None of that mattered. Alistair had returned.

"I'm sorry," he murmured, tucking a chunk of her hair behind her ear. His touch was airy, careful, the tip of his claws barely brushing her skin. "Curses. They're fickle, like your Fates."

Niera shook her head. "I don't understand." She took in the sight of his tail—his tail!—urgency roaring in her head. "You were able to break the curse. But…but…"

His tail flapped again. "Breaking the curse meant returning to my true form. A form I can't change. Merfolk are merfolk. We aren't shifters."

"No," she whispered, cupping his jaw and forcing him to look at her as he tried to avoid her gaze. "No. This can't be it. There's got to be something we missed. Something *I* missed."

"Niera, I would have sacrificed my world underwater to be with you. That was my plan. Unfortunately, for the curse to be broken, I had to return to my original form. I sacrificed us to save you."

Niera ground her teeth together, frustration rising. She turned her face to the sky and shouted, "This is your idea of a joke? Complete my hundredth match or be destined to live alone? Then you steal the one fated to me *by your own hands*!"

"Niera, I don't have much time. I can't stay out of the water long."

A cold wind whipped through the dunes, stinging her eyes as they filled with tears. She fought back a sob, pressing her cheek into Alistair's hand as he framed her face.

"I want to thank you for everything you've done to help me. I don't know why this moon was different, but the only thing I can think of is it was because of you. This bond we share, it'll be something I'll treasure forever, even if it ends with us here. Tonight." He wiped a stray tear from her cheek with the back of his finger. "I knew from the first time I touched you there was something different about you. Not only did you steal my thoughts and my breath, but I realized last night that you stole my heart as well. Love at first sight."

"And I pushed you away." She shook her head and sniffled. "I was scared. Seeing our lifelines entwined frightened me, but I wanted nothing more than to pursue what the Fates prescribed for us. I wanted you by my side."

Alistair guided her head close to his, pressing their foreheads together. His skin was cold, like ice, not the warm human skin she'd snuggled against only yesterday.

"I'll forever keep you in my heart. And I'll forever be in yours."

She combed her fingers through his hair, the salty film making the strands coarse. "You have my heart." Closing her eyes, she whispered, "Kiss me before you leave."

"I wouldn't dream of leaving without a kiss."

Niera swallowed back a relentless sob. Alistair kissed her, a breezy caress along her lips that left an essence of salt.

The sea salt didn't harm her.

He swept his tongue between her lips, impressing the truth of his declaration behind the delicacy of his sweet kiss.

She clung to him, never wanting to let him go. Their time was short, too short, unfairly short.

Curses and Fates.

The sob squeezed past her barriers and tangled between their tongues.

Alistair leaned back, tracing her bottom lip with his thumb.

A speck of white fluttered down between them to land on the back of his hand.

Niera squinted.

The tiny crystalline shape melted slowly.

She looked up at the sky and the gray clouds that had taken it over. A second flake landed on her nose, a cold kiss that shot heat through her veins.

Alistair stiffened and gasped, falling onto his back. His body bowed off the sand, tremors convulsing his muscles.

Frantic, Niera rushed her hands over his chest, trying to keep him calm while her heart raced. "What's going on? Alistair? What's happening?"

Veins bulged from his neck. He bared his teeth behind taut lips, his claws sinking into the sand on either side of him.

She looked down at his restless tail, flapping and smacking into the sand.

Then, it shimmered. Dimly at first, growing brighter and brighter until Niera was forced to look away. She clung to Alistair's shoulders, waiting for him to open his eyes, to look at her, to find strength in her nearness.

A strangled cry sieved through his teeth.

A flash of light shoved her away and her back smacked into the sand dune.

Then, all was silent except for the waves scraping over the beach, and a quiet meow.

Holly padded to Alistair's unmoving form and tentatively

licked his temple. Niera scrambled to his side, checking for a pulse, and sighed when her fingers were greeted with a strong, steady beat.

"Alistair?"

The purple-gray tint to his skin faded, leaving the familiar sun-kissed hue. His face smoothed, the inhumanly sharp angles softening.

When his eyelids fluttered open, she found herself staring into familiar indigo orbs, pupil and all.

Alistair reached up to her face, the webbing and claws gone. His brow furrowed before he lifted his head off the sand and looked down.

Niera followed his gaze.

And gasped, jerking around and squeezing her eyes shut.

Alistair laughed, his hand on her arm. "I would have warned you if I realized what had happened. We don't keep pants in our wardrobes."

"Apparently," she squeaked.

Holly released a strange sound she swore sounded like a laugh. *"You got yourself a good one, Niera."*

"Ooh, you sly little feline." She scooped the cat up and tucked her against her chest. "You can't whip up some pants, can you?"

"Do I look like a magician?"

"Whenever you cats are around, things go crazy," Alistair said, scanning the beach. "What was the difference this full moon? Care to share?"

Holly purred as Niera scratched her head. *"You hadn't crossed paths with Niera yet. You couldn't leave until that happened."*

"She said we had to cross paths before you could leave." She placed Holly on her lap and shimmied out of her jacket.

"Here. It's not much, but it should cover your parts until we can get you home."

Alistair caught her hand as she held out the jacket. She looked at him, her face on fire. Nothing could distract her from the love in his eyes, an emotion that resonated deep in her marrow.

"I don't know how to explain this"—he jutted his chin to his legs—"but I'm not taking a thing for granted. Come home with me. Stay with me from here on out. We'll figure something out to counter the spell on you, but this, all of this, brought us together. Wishes, magic, curses, spells. We got through it together."

Niera reached over and slung her arms around Alistair's neck.

"You're right. We did this together, and together we'll be."

CHAPTER TWELVE

Christmas Eve

"Deck the halls with boughs of holly!"

Niera laughed, hanging the last ornament on the Christmas tree as friends old and new sang wildly off key to the music playing over the speaker. Alistair snaked an arm around her waist, pressing a kiss to her lips as he handed her another cup of spiked eggnog. She had no idea what was in the drink, but it went down nice and smooth, leaving her warm and tingly.

"Are we ready to light the tree?" Alistair asked.

"I think they're having too much fun singing."

"Trying to sing and wrecking our eardrums while they're at it."

They sipped their eggnog, watching the spectacle before them. Danny and Annise draped in colored garlands, elf-ear headbands settled haphazardly on their heads. Brayden and his new girlfriend swaying as they sang loudly, wearing matching Santa hats and elf slippers. Batches of cookies left the air smelling sweet, with a hint of pine from the tree. A fire flickered in the electric fireplace, where stockings dangled off deer-shaped hangers and a pine garland boasted twinkling fairy lights. Holly and her tabby friend, Masey, lay stretched out over the sofa, tails swishing softly, eyes half-mast.

Niera never knew a Christmas like this, and she anticipated many more to come.

"Guys, the tree?" Alistair asked, his inquiry was drowned out by the cringe-worthy karaoke. He chuckled and shook his head, tugging her closer. "Too much spike in the 'nog."

"So it seems." She rested her head against his shoulder. "We can always light it ourselves."

His shaded gaze lowered to hers. "We can."

"And then we can slip away…"

His smile grew. "Into the kitchen."

Niera pressed up on her toes, teasing his jaw with her lips. "Alone."

"They'll be too busy singing."

She nuzzled her nose to his cheek. "They'll never realize we're gone."

"Until half the sugar cookies are gone."

"Exactly."

Alistair stole a kiss that left her entire body a tingling mess.

"Let's save the tree for when our drunken friends come to their senses. In the meantime, I do have a little something for you. An early present."

"Really?"

Excitement flooded her as she folded her hand in his and let him lead her into the kitchen. He placed their eggnog mugs on the counter and faced her.

Answers to questions never came in a straightforward manner. But curses weren't known for being straightforward. Instead, Alistair came to forgive the mischievous Sherwood cats for keeping him from the sea, understanding now the reason why.

Niera had a vision shortly after the events from the full moon that explained, in a twisted, nonsensical way, that the lifting of Alistair's curse allowed them both to accept each other for who they were. Since they both declared love before the first snowflake hit, it satisfied her quota of one hundred matches, and granted Alistair his true desire—to live in the human world with her.

Holly confessed to planting the wishing coin in the planter after being refused a bowl of milk. Her nefarious friend did, in fact, have a milk addiction. She also confessed to waiting for Niera's arrival in Cat's Paw Cove so she could adopt her human, er, fae.

As for the spell cast by the sea fae?

Love truly did conquer all.

Years of struggle, days of challenges, had brought them both to this point in time. This moment.

A moment where they were together and nothing could tear them apart.

Alistair dug a hand into the pocket of his khaki pants and retrieved a small velvet bag. He loosened the ties.

"What is that?"

"This." He lowered to his knee and retrieved a gold ring with a large princess-cut diamond. "You know I fumble over words when it comes to you, so I'll make this simple. I don't ever want to live a day where I can't come home to you. Where I can't imagine sharing my life with you. We were blessed with a special bond, a perfect match, and I will never take that, or you, for granted. So, I want to make it official. Will you marry me, Niera Blair?"

"Marry? You?"

He nodded, his smile faltering.

Niera threw herself at Alistair, wrapping her arms around his neck as tears welled in her eyes. "Yes!"

"You had me worried there." He held her close, finding her lips and kissing her until all that existed was a woodland fae and a former merman in a sea of happiness.

When they finally broke from the kiss, Alistair brought her hand around and slid the ring on her finger, placing a kiss to her knuckles. Niera admired the sparkling diamond, then lifted her eyes to the man who promised his love for the rest of their lives with that very stone.

"I came to Cat's Paw Cove anticipating my departure. Never in all my life could I have imagined the whirlwind adventures this little town had in store for me." Cupping his face between her hands, she smiled. "The love I'd find. As much as I disliked that first day, I will never wish for things to have happened any differently. And with all the wishing that went on, I think it's fair to call this particular Christmas a Wishmas."

Alistair chuckled. "My woodland fae's Wishmas." He curled his fingers in her hand and drew her closer. "I love you, Niera."

"I love you, Alistair. And I'm looking forward to many years of happiness here in Cat's Paw Cove, with you."

THE END

ACKNOWLEDGMENT

A huge thank you to Wynter and Catherine for allowing me to write in this amazing town of Cat's Paw Cove! The journey was amazing and I can't wait to do it again. A shout out to Raina and Kerry, catching those little details that make things flow smoothly. And a gracious thanks to all of my readers! Enjoy the magic!

ABOUT THE AUTHOR

Born and raised a Jersey girl with easy access to NYC, Kira was never short on ideas for stories. She started writing at the tender age of 11, and her passion for creating worlds exploded from that point on. Romance came later, but since then, all of her heroes and heroines find their happily ever after, even if it takes a good fight, or ten, to get there.

Kira resides in Central Florida with her husband, four children, two bunnies, and a guinea pig. She works part-time as a nurse when she's not writing or traveling between sports, other activities, or her characters' worlds.

Kira loves to hear from readers! Find her at:

Website and Newsletter: www.kiranyte.com
Contact: kiranyteauthor@gmail.com